DON'T LOOK BACK

AND OTHER STORIES

KATE SHEERAN SWED

To Chace
Because you know why

CONTENTS

The Rest is Silence   1
Windfall   11
Rare   34
Don't Look Back   38
Insubstantial   51
Interplanetary Ghost Rushers   54
mBedi   68
You Always Had a Thing for Silver Linings   83

Newsletter   87
Also By Kate Sheeran Swed   89
About the Author   91

THE REST IS SILENCE

I didn't bother to sand the plank of wood that's holding up my protest sign, an oversight I regret as soon as the splinter sinks into my hand. We're packed along Broadway like it's some kind of messed-up New Year's Eve, only we're shouting down our new evil overlords instead of counting down with an overhyped disco ball.

Last time we did this, news drones dipped and circled through the crowd, but BurnerCorp just dismantled the first amendment. Today's sky is clear.

I'm not a klutz or anything like that, but the splinter bite jars the sign out of my grip. My first thought is of the poor stranger whose head's about to get clocked.

Luckily, my kid brother Benny's got quick reflexes. He catches the sign, holds it up with a grin like he just scored a soccer goal, and hefts it back to me.

Benny's only ten, young enough to think this whole Mega-Corp-Government-Buyout situation is going to blow over on its own.

Me? I'm sixteen. And I'm a girl.

I know better.

Mom turns to make sure we're OK. She's got dark half-moons stamped under her eyes, but I think it makes her protest slogan—STICK IT TO THE FEES—look even more badass.

"All good, Jodi?" she mouths—or maybe shouts. I don't know, because the thunder of voices is reverberating from skyscraper to skyscraper, chants and songs mixing together as they rise. I imagine the BurnerCorp President standing in the window of his corner office, smoking a cigar and laughing maniacally while he watches us march.

I give Mom a thumbs-up. All good.

As soon as I do, the lights in Times Square blink out. It's enough to send a hush through the crowd. By the time people rally their chants again, every screen in Times Square is filled with Old White Dude.

There are a lot of screens in Times Square.

"Compromise," the old dude says, his voice ringing through the square. I'm rolling my eyes already. "Compromise is something BurnerCorp values. We've heard you. And we're responding."

Oh, this is rich. I look at Benny, but he mimics my thumbs-up from before, like he thinks we just won a battle.

I'll explain to him where he went wrong, later.

I look at Mom. I'm expecting to exchange an eye-roll, a grimace, something. But she's staring at the closest screen, neck cricked back, the reflection of Old Dude flickering in her eyes. Her lips are parted.

She looks...hopeful.

"You can all start working for BurnerCorp today," the dude says. When I look away from Mom and back to the screen, I find myself inexplicably riveted by his eyebrows. They stick out in every direction, white mixed so perfectly with the black that it looks like stripes.

I'm thinking a rich guy like that could probably afford a mini golden comb to groom those caterpillars.

"The only line in your job description," he continues, "is silence."

I laugh out loud.

The sound echoes across the square.

I'm not embarrassed to be alone. I'm pissed.

"For every day of total silence you complete, Burner-Corp will pay you in gold. Accept a WordBuster bracelet from one of our representatives, and payment will automatically be transferred to your account each day. No strings attached."

Like hell. The whole thing is a string. It's a manacle, is what it is.

I see orange-uniformed BurnerCorp sellouts waving from the curb, a whole line of them appearing as though they teleported here. Each of them's cradling an oversized basket in their hands, and I can see the rubber rings of orange bracelets heaped inside.

Mom's fixated on the screen. She licks her lips.

The woman next to her whispers to herself. Another guy frowns, twisting his hands together nervously. Most of the people around me are shifting their feet.

These people are thinking of accepting the dude's offer.

He gives the proposal a second to sink in before he drops the cherry right on top. "Parents, we at BurnerCorp know you face particularly trying economic circumstances. For every child under the age of twelve in your household, you may collect additional gold without the requirement of the child's silence."

And just like that, Mom lowers her badass sign.

BURNERCORP BOUGHT THE GOVERNMENT FOR, I don't know, billions. Like the whole country was some kind of petty competition they needed to dismantle. Still, they must have been dropping gold in the piggy for a long time to make it happen.

I don't know how they maneuvered it. I just know we woke up to the fees.

School fees, curfew fees, bike fees, park fees, grocery fees, sidewalk fees, bus fees, pet fees, you get my drift. Fees, fees, fees, fees, fees.

We outgrew our winter coats.

We stopped going to school.

My brother was always shivering.

MOM RETURNS from collecting her bracelet and meets my stare head on. "I get it, Jodi," she says, while Benny sits down in the street, abandoned signs fanned out around him on the pavement, and opens some book about space, "but what am I supposed to do?"

"Stick to your convictions?" I say.

Mom looks at Benny, who might as well be on Jupiter right now. He's got the hood of his sweatshirt pulled tight around his head, arms wrapped around his knees as he reads. He needs a coat. And more meat on his growing-boy bones.

Mom hands me a bracelet.

I guess I'm selling out, too.

SCHOOL USED TO BE LOUD. Music blaring and clashing from at least ten devices, personal drones zipping down the hall trying to trip someone before getting confiscated. Lockers slamming, high fives resounding, insults called back and forth.

The lockers still slam, but that's about it. Definitely no high fives. Definitely no music. And no voices.

We're like a herd of zombies, biting our cheeks to keep from saying how messed up this is because our moms are hungry, our baby brothers are cold, and if we're here instead of home it means we're being paid to shut the hell up.

Getting here was weird, too, the city hushed. Oh, there are still people talking; but they're mostly dressed in suits, BurnerCorp orange more often than not. If they don't need the extra gold, they're not saying much I want to hear, anyway.

I meet my friend Ty on the way to social studies. I haven't seen him in months. He slings an arm around my shoulder and opens his mouth, then mimes like he lost his voice and can't figure out why. I point to the bracelet on his wrist, and he slaps a palm to his forehead like *Oh, right. Thaaaaat.*

Ty's cute, I don't know, but mostly he's just nice. He's an inch or two shorter than me, so his arm's propped up at an angle over my shoulder as we shuffle, walking-dead-like, into the classroom.

The teacher is new. All the teachers are new. They wear orange BurnerCorp jackets, which means they're allowed to talk. I guess they get paid enough to compensate for that missing gold.

This guy looks like he could be Old White Dude's cousin, except the striped eyebrows. He's got patches of red on his cheeks, a mole next to his nose.

BurnerCorp orange isn't his color, but hey, we've all got problems.

As soon as we're seated, Teacher Guy just starts talking. No need to quiet the class, I guess.

"The downfall of modern society began in the year 2054," he begins, and I clench my fists so hard my knuckles crack. Next to me, Ty's already shaking his head because he knows what Teacher Guy's about to say.

"2054 was the year the Disruptives grew violent," Teacher Guy says. He's talking like that was a decade ago instead of a year, something distant that we didn't all live through. He keeps droning on, but the rush in my ears is drowning him out.

Doesn't matter. I've heard this BurnerCorp fairy tale before. But everyone knows the Disruptives were framed for those bombings. I know it especially, because my sister was one of the people who got framed.

My fingers hurt from squeezing. I feel Ty trying to catch my eye, but my vision's a tunnel.

"You're wrong," I say. I don't know which part of the fake history Teacher Guy was up to. BurnerCorp's whole schtick is based on the lie that they were forced to save us from ourselves.

As soon as I speak, my bracelet vibrates. A pair of lights turn red.

No pay today.

"Young lady," Teacher Guy says, sounding sympathetic, "you cannot be blamed for your upbringing. But I'm here to set the record straight. For all of you."

"Do you believe the lies you tell?" I ask, because whatever, I've already broken my silence for the day. Might as well make the most of it.

"Please," he says, like he wants to save my soul, "be reasonable. Just listen to our side of the story."

"Your side is the only side anyone can hear," I say, "the rest is just silence."

Teacher Dude blinks. Then he walks to the door, opens it.

He doesn't have to say anything else. I gather my stuff, throw Ty the sassiest wink I can manage, and show myself out.

Mom hides her disappointment when I show up at home early with my bracelet blinking red.

When Benny comes home shivering, I'm disappointed in myself, too.

"Today we'll review the list of heroes who put their lives on the line to capture Disruptives," Teacher Guy says. His eyes flicker to me, I think, but I have my hands folded on my desk. I think about Benny, and how a few days of silence can buy a new coat. Some extra food. Maybe a ball to bounce around.

Thinking like that must be how Mom sleeps at night.

"Adam Corning," Teacher Guy says. He must've looked up my family; he's baiting me, because Adam Corning is the BurnerCorp crony cop who arrested my sister Jen.

There were hundreds of these guys, and Teacher Guy chooses Adam Corning to talk about.

I drop my book on the floor. Teacher Guy jumps.

Ty's watching me.

"Hero," Teacher Guy says.

"Murderer," I respond.

My bracelet blinks red.

He doesn't kick me out today. Instead, it's detention. Two hours of sitting at a desk while he sits placidly at his, sipping on the coffee that makes his breath stink, his already ruddy cheeks flushing with triumph.

MOM'S WAITING at the kitchen table when I get home. I sit down next to her, and for a while we just stare kind of bleakly at the walls. The paint is peeling, and the only decorations we've got are some pieces of kid art Mom taped to the fridge so long ago that I can't remember if they're Benny's or mine.

Mom slips a piece of paper across the table to me.

Jodi, it reads, written in one of Benny's bright red markers, *this could be dangerous.*

I remember sitting at this table with Jen, learning to play poker. We were awful insomniacs, Jen and me. She'd shuffle the cards, impress me with her moves. The flip-flip rhythm of the cards slapping the table, a mug of mint tea to warm my hands.

I was always terrible at bluffing. Still am. "They're rewriting history," I say. I've already forfeited my payment for the day. "How can you stand it?"

Mom shakes her head slowly, pinches her lips together like she doesn't know what to tell me. All I want is the truth. In her voice.

It's complicated, she writes.

Benny, she writes.

"I'm still a kid, too," I say.

Mom flips the marker between her fingers. Could she not find a subtler color? A pen? Anything? She writes, slides the paper over.

Exactly.

TECHNICALLY, Jen's only missing. She could be in one of the BurnerCorp jails we pretend not to know about.

As for me, I'm a practical person. I know my sister isn't coming back.

TY PASSES me a note before social studies.

What's on the menu for today's rebellion?

The funny thing is that when I look at him, he's got an eyebrow lifted like he's asking me a serious question. He hasn't joined me in breaking his silence; no one has.

Mom's right. There really isn't a point. We're kids; we're powerless.

Talk about depressing.

I press a finger to my lips. I'm not messing up today. I'm not muttering a thing. I won't so much as roll my eyes.

Teacher Guy does his best to make my compliance an uphill battle. He's taken me on now, a personal project, all traces of false sympathy vanished. He spends the whole period talking about Adam Corning.

I'm ready for it. I don't make a move.

Ty's giving me the same questioning look he gave me when I was talking back every day. I want to tell him that he needs to choose. Either he's confused because I'm speaking up, or he's confused that I'm *shutting* up.

He can't be confused about both.

Before I can write him a note to that effect, Ty opens his mouth and names Adam Corning a murderer.

His bracelet blinks red.

And just like that, there are two of us.

It's a funny thing about silence. It feeds on itself, I guess. If you never let it in, it can't scare you away.

One day, my brother Benny shows up in my room with the wool blanket from his bed and a pair of fabric scissors. We cut a hole for his head, and we laugh and laugh because when he shrugs it over his shoulders, he looks like a bear cub that shaved its face.

Detention is always full now. I doubt the Old White Dude from the Times Square announcement knows about it. I doubt he'd care if he did. We're just kids. We can't be the only ones whose bracelets light up red every day.

Teacher Guy cares. He cares a lot. And that's a battle worth winning.

One day, Mom shows up. She opens the door to the classroom, ignores Teacher Guy's "May I help you?" and pulls a chair up next to my desk.

And then, we talk.

WINDFALL

No miracle ever picked a guy named Phineas Apple to happen to, I can tell you that much. No sudden lucky breaks to plop my ass in magic school or godly summer camp, or to zap me back in time so my cell phone could scare the shit out of old-fashioned people, and they'd try to burn me at the stake, prompting my dangerous and glorious escape.

In fact, I can say with absolute certainty that miracles run screaming from my presence. I'm the first guy in my family—*ever*—who "gets" to go to a normal-ass school with boring-ass kids. As in, Mom and Dad and Grandma and Grandpa and every single and aunt and uncle and second-cousin-twice-removed? They all went to magic school.

Yup. Chew on that for a sec.

Sure, there's some magic kicking around at Atchfield. The teachers keep it locked up tighter than the liquor, even though it's only the weak, donated shit. Barely strong enough to do more than clean chalk off the boards (the magic, that is; Principal Sanders' vodka could strip lacquer. Not that I know firsthand). But ever since a legendary figure named Timmy MacLeod somehow managed to magick chalk tattoos across the football team's foreheads, the teachers aren't taking chances.

Thing about guys like me and Timmy Mac is, we don't sit around to wait on miracles or windfalls. We shake our own trees.

And sometimes when you shake a tree, you wind up on the bench outside the principal's office waiting for a good clean scolding.

I literally never noticed this kid Grant Harper before we were side-by-side on said bench. Like, I seriously did not know he existed. To the point where, when we got back to math class later, the kid was sitting *next* to me. That's how I am, sometimes.

And that's how noticeable Grant was back then, to be fair. Scrawny kid, too-big glasses, gleaming white sneakers. You might glance in his general direction, and those sneakers would blind the hell out of you, so you'd look away to avoid permanent damage to your corneas.

So we were sitting outside the principal's office, right, and this kid had his butt so close to the edge that it had to be digging right into the bone. Knees clenched tight, palms locked between them, a thunderstorm of sobs erupting every few seconds.

I watched him for a minute or two, because it wasn't like I was going anywhere. Finally, enough time passed that I decided to say, "If you don't relax, Principal Sanders is gonna fry you alive and eat you for lunch."

Grant swiveled his head without moving his palms from between his knees. He'd been crying so hard that there were drops of water on the lenses of his glasses. How that even happens, that his eyeballs could squirt tears so hard they literally soaked the lenses of his glasses, I still have no idea.

Grant said, "What?" and his voice was so snot-clogged that I almost gagged.

But I still figured I'd help him out. That's the kind of guy I am. "I don't know what you did, kid," I said, "but whatever it was, you gotta sit back. Arch an eyebrow, if you can squeak it past those glasses. Smirk. Show them you don't care."

"Oh." Grant sat up straight, shook out his hands, and folded his arms across his chest, giving him the impression of a bird perching on a pole. "I'm not in trouble. My uncle died. They just told me."

"Well, fuck," I said. "I'm sorry to hear that."

Of course, me being me, the door opened right as I said that, so Principal Sanders had an excuse to turn up the menacing-glare dial as she looked down at me. "Mr. Apple," she said, "*language.*"

I saluted. "Right, Colonel Sanders," I said. "Sorry, ma'am. Won't happen again ma'am."

She sighed, but I knew better than to believe it. I'm hilarious. "In my office, Mr. Apple."

And then her eyes shifted to Grant. And I am not shitting you, her expression melted. She went from vulture to grandma in the snap of a finger. "Mr. Harper. Stay there as long as you need. Let us know if there's anything we can do."

I didn't hear his response, because I was already slumping into the chair across from the Desk of Doom. I'm the only one who calls it that. I've got a trademark pending. The Desk of Doom was Principal Sanders' round monstrosity of a desk. It looked like they murdered one of those ginormous trees in California to get it there.

Anyway, I slumped into the chair and folded my arms. I had this really good way of spreading out my legs and lifting the most infuriating smirk.

"Mr. Apple," Sanders said as she closed the door, all

vulture again. Her hair was long and braided, gray roots peeking out beneath the blond. No buns or anything, but still. Vulture. "Do you know why you're here?"

"I let a Phoenix into the file room."

I had to hand it to her; Sanders had a worthy eyebrow arch of her own. "Excuse me?"

"Didn't find that yet? OK. Then I have no idea why I'm here."

Sanders reached into her Drawer of Confiscated Shit (another pending TM) and set a box on the table.

I was generally used to having the upper hand in these conversations, but I'll admit I took a minute to stare.

"Do you know what this is, Mr. Apple?"

Here's the thing about principal visits. If you own up, you have to face the consequences. Detention, whatever. Suspension, ugh, a few days enduring fatherly lectures at home. If you lie, you might be able to evade punishment—probably not, if you're me—but you risk never getting your shit back.

I really needed to get this particular shit back.

"This, Mr. Apple," said Principal Sanders—correctly interpreting my silence as consent, damnit—"is an unauthorized magical artifact."

"I mean, not really," I said. I noticed myself sitting up in the chair and immediately re-slumped, but the maneuver was too awkward and now Principal Sanders had *my* patented smirk on *her* face, which meant I'd screwed up royally.

So what did I do? I kept running my mouth, of course. Because I never know when to shut the hell up. "It'll *be* a magical artifact someday, but it isn't one *yet* because it has no magic to run it. So it's not against the rules, unless someone magicks it into working like a magical artifact is supposed to....work."

Unfortunately, Principal Sanders' smirk just deepened. The woman must have cracked into that liquor cabinet early today. She pressed a button on the side of the box, and a pair of dice tumbled out. They did a little dance to show all four of their sides, then twirled and landed. Snake eyes.

"Not only is this an unauthorized artifact, but it is a gambling device using *weighted* dice. Mr. Apple."

It wasn't my best invention. It wasn't even a good invention. It was just a way of getting some cash, or some magic—both, either—to fund better inventions.

"Some of the eight-year-olds used their milk magic to get this going after they found it in the lavatory," Principal Sanders explained.

"Then they're smart enough to know this is a better use for their magic then spelling milk to be more nutritious or whatever the hell their parents—"

"*Language*, Mr. Apple." Sanders cleared her throat. "The artifact was confiscated by a teacher who found the dice displaying their backsides to the children in a most unpleasant way."

Heh. OK, so it wasn't a *bad* invention. Kind of funny, really. Mooning dice.

"I will be posting it to your father immediately," Sanders said.

Cue audible groan. My father's the kind of useless guy whose head is jammed so far into the clouds that you have to wave a flare in front of his face just to keep him from dying of starvation. And yet, somehow, there was never any space in his head for other people's dreams.

"That's all, Mr. Apple."

"What, no detention?"

"I can't increase maximum detention without cutting into class time."

Right. I got to my feet, summoning as much grace as I could muster to sweep Principal Sanders a bow.

I think even she knew it was a reach.

I WAS MENTALLY PREPARING a phone call to my father, to preempt the arrival of the dice box, which was why I didn't see Grant until I was about five seconds from walking into him. I'm pretty sure I wouldn't have seen him at all except that he was out on the quad between the academic building and the dorms, and he was surrounded by a semi-circle of admiring students.

He was not the kind of kid you expected to have a circle of admirers, especially with his eyes all red-rimmed and his cheeks still streaked with tears. And yet, here he was.

Never one to miss a spectacle, or an opportunity to post-pone a call to my father, I stepped into the fringes of the circle.

"...won't be at Atchfield much longer, I guess, will you, Grant?" a pretty girl was saying, looking sad. I'm only guessing that I learned his name around this time. Artistic license. "You'll go off to another school."

A pretty girl was sad that this gawky Grant kid might be leaving school? Curiouser and curiouser.

"My uncle went to Kennbire," Grant said, but without much enthusiasm. "I guess maybe that's what he wanted me to do."

At the word *Kennbire*, I edged so far into the circle that I was actually *in* the circle, and suddenly Grant and the pretty girl were both staring at me. Grant had an envelope in his hand, and a wooden box covered in carved birds at his feet. The girl was looking at Grant, but the other kids had their attention locked on the box.

Dead uncle. Kennbire.

Ding ding ding. See, Kennbire is one of those wand-waving schools that other kids get hauled off to when their family is lousy with magic. But I don't think I'm representing it right. Kennbire is *the* school, like the high school Harvard of magic. Hoity toity, sure, but also the kind of place where magical inventions—like mine—get lab time instead of detention time.

"I inherited some magic from my uncle," Grant explained.

I tried to look surprised, like I hadn't already pieced it together, and I'm a pretty good actor so of course the kid bought it. Plus, I'd had the benefit of talking to him before the crowd. Which meant I could interpret the shaky smile and the way he clenched the letter in his fist, like he just wanted to get away.

An important part of making one's own miracles is in grasping opportunity.

"I'm really sorry about your uncle," I said, trying to keep the fuck-word out of it this time, in case it should offend Grant Harper's delicate sensibilities or summon a teacher out of thin air.

Grant's eyes filled up with tears, and just like that, I was in.

"Maybe we should give the kid some space," I said, and because most of the other kids at school were a little afraid of me, they fucked off, and I stayed with Grant.

He watched them go, and then he sat down on the grass and started murdering it by the handful, ripping up chunks and scattering them into the wind. I watched him for a bit before sitting down next to him. "Want to talk about it?" I asked.

"What's there to talk about? I had an uncle. Now I have his magic. I've had it for half an hour, and already everyone else knows what I should do with it."

"How much magic is it?" I asked.

He shrugged. "My uncle was Reginald Haynes."

Holy fuuuuuuuuu— "As in the Sorcerer General of the United States?"

Grant nodded, looking miserable. "He always said I had fire in me. No one else ever said that."

No shit. "I know you're overwhelmed by all this," I said in my best guidance-counselor imitation. "If you want, I can help you."

"How are you going to help me, Phineas?"

"You know my name?"

Grant demonstrated a genuinely not-sucky eyebrow arch of his own. "Um, yeah."

Gratifying. "OK, then call me Phin or I will throw you in the fountain. I know an investment opportunity that could help you," I told him, and because the kid immediately got this gassy look on his face like the way he was looking at the others, I added, "and it'll buy you time to decide what to do with your lucky stroke."

Grant's scowl deepened. "How?"

"There's a wishing well upstate, near Ithaca. It needs refurbishing."

Am I good at bullshitting, or am I good at bullshitting?

"You contribute to the refurbishment," I continued, "and it'll pay you back in twice the magic."

"How do you know about this?"

I coughed. "My dad's kind of Benjamin Apple."

Grant lost the scowl in favor of loose-jaw amazement. "What are you doing in this school?"

My dad sucks, that's what I was doing in that school. But I couldn't exactly use Dad's name for leverage one second and discredit him the next, now could I? "What are *you* doing in this school?"

Grant's creepy owl-eyes collapsed back to their normal shape, thank god. "My mom wouldn't accept any magic from my uncle. Said we'll make our own way and thank you very much."

Benjamin Apple subject effectively evaded. "So, what do you say?" I asked. "Want to be a magical billionaire?"

"What's in it for you?"

"I want to help you," I said. Then, I paused. For drama. "And maybe fifteen percent commission? As a finders fee."

Grant sat up straight. No fool, him. "Ten percent," he said.

"It's a deal."

And that's how I convinced Grant Harper to hand me his magical fortune.

THE WINDOWS at Atchfield were laughably easy to open. I'd learned that in my first year, when Timmy MacLeod and I slipped out to dye the fountain red. We'd been hoping everyone would think it was blood and go looking for a body. Turned out most of them thought it was wine and had to go to the infirmary.

Now, after class and dinner and a blah blah lecture from my father on responsibility that was riddled with physics-defying metaphors involving my own bootstraps, I finally slid down the dormitory drainpipe with Grant Harper's magical fortune in my backpack—cozied up against a select few of my own inventions—and the future wide open before me.

Grant Harper didn't even want his magical fortune.

I was doing Grant Harper a favor.

I was thinking so much about that favor, in fact, that I seemingly summoned Grant Harper out of midair. One second I was booking it toward the wrought iron gates, the next I was skidding to a stop to avoid bolting straight into the skinny guy, kicking up dust everywhere and threatening to give up my position to every night-owl teacher in the place.

"What the hell?" I said, breathing hard because gym class is for losers, but also because Grant Harper's sudden appearance had scared the bejeezus out of me.

"What are you doing?" Grant asked.

"What am *I* doing?"

"What are you, Phineas Apple, doing leaving campus in the middle of the night with what I can only assume is my magic in your backpack?"

I clamped my teeth together. "It's Phin," I ground out.

"OK, Phin. Same question."

The kid had more guts than I initially gave him credit for.

"Isn't it obvious?" I said, beginning to catch my balance. "I have to take the magic to the wishing well."

"You're walking there?"

"Well, yeah."

"It's like a hundred miles."

"Then, like, I'd better get going," I said. "You can cover for me."

"No way," Grant Harper said, and that's when I noticed:

he was wearing his backpack and a pair of huge clompy hiking boots with pristine toes.

The kid had anticipated my move.

The kid was going to come with me.

"You shouldn't travel alone with that much magic," he said. "There are bandits."

"Bandits? Like the wild west?" I squinted one eye and made a gun shape with my right thumb and index, which did not look or feel as cool as it had in my head. But I was already committed to the gag. No sense in backing down. "Hand over your witchy spells little boys, or I'll pop a hole in your big toe!"

Grant adjusted his pack calmly. "There are bandits. My uncle told me so."

"They wouldn't dare mess with Phin the Terror!"

Grant stared at me until I holstered the thumb and index. "You don't need to come," I said. "I'll be back in a few days with double the magic, and you'll be so rich you can quit school and join the circus."

Grant didn't call attention to the nonsensical nature of my claim. He just said, "I'm coming with you."

Around this time, my spidey sense started sending up flares. Because let's be honest, no one's handing out extra trust to a guy like me. Even Timmy MacLeod, before he got expelled, knew to watch his back for "Kick Me" signs when I was in the vicinity.

Grant Harper might be standing here all nickel-eyed and earnest, pretending to be out for some grief-squashing adventure, but it didn't add up.

Whatever his game was, I figured I'd have plenty of time to Sherlock it out of him before we got too far. And then? Well, the road from Tarrytown to Ithaca would be a three-day trek, at best. A lot could happen in three days. People could get separated. Lost, even. Maybe a handsome, intelligent, talented young man with a magical fortune in his pack would go off to collect wood for a campfire, and maybe instead of making it back to the campsite, he'd hightail it to Kennbire to make a case for his admission.

A lot could happen in three days.

AT FIRST, I did my best to get the kid to leave on his own. It was nearly eleven when we left, and a skinny kid like that, I figured he'd be exhausted during the first hour.

But it turned out that Grant Harper took gym class as seriously as he took everything else, and that he had an annoying amount of energy for a kid who was up in the middle of the night for semi-nefarious purposes.

"I can't believe we left school," he kept saying, leading me to believe that this was, in his experience, a fully nefarious purpose. "I can't believe we just walked out the gates and no one saw. When do you think they'll notice we're gone? Do you think they'll call the police?"

This was the kind of thinking I needed to squash. A kid like Grant would start thinking his parents were worried, phone them all on his own, and cry the truth to his mommy before anyone else had even searched beyond the boys' bathroom.

"I think we'd better camp," I said, mostly to distract him. We'd been heading north along the state road with the Hudson to our left. Out of sight, if not out of smell, the rivery, radioactive aroma thick in the air. For the last hour, we'd been surrounded by State Forest trees. Tomorrow we'd cross the river by ferry—every adventure needs a ferry— and head west.

"We're too close to Atchfield," Grant said.

"Yeah, well, I've got blisters."

Without waiting for an answer, I barreled my way into the trees and found a spot that looked good for a nap. I propped myself up against a tree trunk, folded my arms, and closed my eyes. It took a while to fall asleep, since Grant insisted on reading on his phone for hours on end, burning the other side of my eyelids with LED torture. After a while, though, my pretending became reality and I passed out.

In the morning, the full annoyance of Grant's presence became clear.

First of all, Grant was and is a morning person. Chatter, chatter, chatter. Even after a night sleeping with our backs against trees, with fucking owls hooting and elves stalking, and whatever the hell else lives in forests. Morning people have absolutely no decency, if you ask me.

Second, Grant is practical.

"I need coffee," I said as we packed up our stuff.

"We can't risk stopping," he said, looking scandalized. "We're barely five miles from school. We shouldn't talk to anyone."

"I need coffee," I repeated.

"If you stop for coffee, I'll take my magic and go back to Atchfield."

"Bluffing. That would spoil your devious plan."

Grant just blinked at me.

I considered suggesting he go out for drama club.

We didn't stop. And it was a good thing, too. If we had, I'd have spilled scalding coffee right in the kid's lap.

～

NIGHT NUMBER TWO, state park number two, and I swear my feet were going to fall off. It wasn't like we had to cook camp food or make a fire to stay warm or shit like that. Grant declared us far enough from Atchfield to eat McDonald's— though I think it was mostly because I hadn't brought any food, because I'd been picturing eating McDonald's—before we snuck into the forest.

My feet felt like blocks of concrete. The straps on my pack were wearing blisters onto my shoulder blades, and I was beginning to think that I, Phineas Apple, might have been a bit coddled. I took my shoes off and rubbed my feet, and wished to hell for one cold sip of beer.

Grant on the other hand just sighed, shuffled around for a while, then settled. I still had no clue what the kid's deal was. I half expected him to throttle me in the night, steal back his magic fortune, and make a run for it.

Whatever his plan was, I was beginning to think he needed me in order to carry it out. For what purpose— unless he had a spell to revive his uncle from the dead and I was here as the sacrificial asshole—I could not begin to guess.

I was dropping off to sleep when the familiar blue blaze of his screen shimmered against my eyelids. I opened them to find Grant with his phone an inch from his face.

"You should conserve the battery," I said.

"I've got one of those travel chargers."

I shrugged and shut my eyes. Worst case, I'd harangue Grant until he allowed us time to charge in a Starbucks tomorrow. No way this road wouldn't pass a Starbucks eventually.

I hadn't unearthed the kid's plot yet, but the time would soon come when I'd need to ditch him, anyway. Maybe a Starbucks would be just the ticket. Pop inside the bathroom, find a window, maybe hitch a ride and voila. See you later, kid.

I did my best to pass out, and you'd think it'd be easy after tripling my ten thousand steps for the day, but Grant didn't put the damn phone away. He just kept staring and scrolling and staring and scrolling until I got up and snatched the phone out of his hand. "Get some sleep," I said.

He swiped for it, but I kept it out of reach. As I passed it above my head, a snippet of the article he'd been reading caught my eye.

"Surefire Spells for the Self-Conscious Sorcerer," I read. "What is this?"

Grant took the opportunity to grab his phone and stuff it into the pocket of his sweatshirt. "Nothing."

I crossed my arms and waited, teacher style.

"Kennbire's in Ithaca," he said, still mumbling.

I put on my best 'Oh-really?' expression. Tilt of the head, pinch of the lip, furrow of the brow. Easy to overdo, though. Practice well in advance.

"And you're afraid you won't make the cut because you're a Self-Conscious Sorcerer?"

"I'm not a sorcerer at all." Grant said. He flopped back against the tree and pulled his knees up to his chest. And for at least the second time, I felt kind of bad for the guy.

I sat down across from him and folded my legs. "All right," I said. "I can show you a couple things."

Grant dragged his hand across his nose, though he hadn't actually been crying. "You go to Atchfield," he said. "What can you show me?"

"I go to Atchfield because my dad's a fuckup who squandered all the family magic when I was twelve," I said, without quite meaning to. Remember what I said about running my mouth? Yeah.

"You should've gone to Kennbire?"

"Or one of the others. Doesn't matter." It did, but Grant didn't need to know that. "Look at this."

I eased the chest out of the backpack and motioned for him to place his palm under the spigot on the side of the box. It was carved in the shape of a bird, so the magic would float right out of the beak. Picturesque as hell.

When Grant had his hand in position, I opened the tap, and a slice of magic flopped onto his palm. I gave it a quick stir with my pinky to test for buoyancy before withdrawing my latest—and second-greatest—invention from the pack.

"A magic wand?" Grant said, his voice tinged with the edge of condescension. Pretty rich, coming from a sorcerer who couldn't even sorcer.

"No," I said. "It's a cheat sheet. I dip it into the magic in your palm, and now you can ask it shit."

"You don't need this."

"Others do."

"You're making inventions to help people?"

"I make inventions to help *me*, kid."

"We're exactly the same age."

"That's right, kid," I said.

"You could have made an invention to steal money, and that would help you," Grant said. "But you made something nice. Phineas Apple made something nice."

I'm not *too* easily offended, but I admit I was starting to bristle at his surprise. "Why not?" I said. "Am I that bad?"

"You ran Jim Archer's underwear up the flag pole."

Because I found him spying on the girls' showers, that's why. "I'll run yours up next, and with you in it, if you keep calling me Phineas."

"You don't have any friends. Not since Timmy got expelled last year."

"I'm a lone wolf. I observe from the sidelines."

"Did you even know my name before the principal's office?"

"Do you want to learn magic, or not?"

He nodded, and glory of all glory, he dropped the Phin-is-a-nice guy subject and settled his attention on my Study Stick (double entendre intended, patent pending). I showed him how to activate it, and how to ask for the spell he wanted. Pretty soon the wand was dancing in midair while he conjured firewood and built a campfire, which I'd have argued against, except it was pleasant to sit with the crackling wood, all the sparks neatly contained by magic.

It wasn't fancy magic, but it was a start.

One last day. One last night. I didn't need to know the kid's angle. I think part of me didn't want to know how he planned to betray me. Tomorrow we'd find a Starbucks, I'd sneak out the window, and I'd ditch him for good.

At least for tonight, I could pretend to have a friend.

I EDGED BACK to consciousness to the feeling of some asshole looming over me. "You're blocking the heat," I said, eyes still closed.

"Hear that, Mer? I'm blocking his heat." The voice was low and loud, and one hundred percent un-Grant like. My eyes flew open to find a huge dude wearing a denim vest with superhero pins covering every inch of the pockets.

You'd think a guy wearing superhero pins would not be rifling through someone else's belongings, and that his accomplice would not have her hand wrapped like a vice around Grant's wrist. But no. This duo must have beaten all those superheroes and collected their pins as trophies.

"This chest looks positively magical," the dude said. "Look at the birds, Mer."

The woman—Mer, apparently—leaned toward the box, pulling poor Grant along as she moved. She stuck her nose against the box's keyhole, gave one great, gurgling inhale, and grinned. "Fortune's worth."

"Hundreds?" the dude asked.

I think you realize by now that I am no saint, but this asshole's greed practically oozed out of him. Desperation is not a look that wears well on most people. I should know.

"Millions," she breathed.

"It'll be more," Grant said.

Initiate palm to face. "Oh, shut up," I said.

"Too late." Mer gave Grant a shake. "What's the story, little stork?"

"Stork," the dude snorted. "You're adept at matching animals to people, Mer. Adept."

"That's a talent to be proud of," I said.

Mer gave Grant another shake, and his glasses rattled off his face. "Tell him," Grant said. "Phin, tell him about the wishing well in Ithaca."

"Oh, this sounds delicious," the dude said. "What wishing well, Phin? Do tell."

"It needs refurbishing," Grant said, before I could shut him up. "We deliver the magic, we come out with double in return. Let us go and we'll cut you in."

For a beat, the bandits just stared at Grant. And then, they burst out laughing.

"Kid," Mer hiccuped, "you've been conned."

Grant blinked. "What?"

And I swear to god, I almost puked in surprise. Because in that moment, when I looked at him, I saw the truth spelled out on his face like a neon sign. All along, the kid was exactly what he seemed to be. Loyal as Lassie. No ulterior motives, no plots, no plans to sacrifice me on the alter of magic.

I tried to tell myself it was a letdown, that I'd begun to think more highly of Grant than that. But the thought rang hollow, even inside my head.

What the hell kind of dumbass puts his faith in a guy like me?

"Ain't no wishing well in Ithaca that'll double a magic fortune," the dude said. "Ain't no wishing well anywhere that'll do that. Only thing in Ithaca is waterfalls, hippies, and that snotty magic school."

Grant shook his head. "No, you're—"

But he cut off when he looked at me. At least, I think that's what he did. I was studying the ground, wondering what kind of weasel Mer would name me. A ground-dwelling rodent of some kind.

What the hell kind of dumbass. Seriously.

"You've been traveling with a snake, kid," Mer said, as if reading my thoughts. Snake. Yeah, that was about right. "I don't know what his plan is, but he sure as hell isn't going to double your fortune."

Grant pulled his spine up straight, and I could tell he was about to do something stupid.

Once in a while, I'm right.

"My uncle was Reginald Haynes," he said. "Let us go, or there'll be an army of cops after you in no time."

At that, the dude actually dropped my backpack—and along with it, the chest of magic. "What I heard," he said, "was that there's an even bigger ransom waiting at the other end of a phone call."

All attention on Grant, I spied—for the first time since our venture together—an opportunity. The chest was right there, at my feet. One dip into that magic, and I could make myself invisible, or super speedy, or anything I wanted.

The door to escape stood wide open. The bandits would ransom Grant to his family. I'd go to Kennbire and use the kid's unwanted fortune—yes, I was still telling myself that—to sail through my magic audition. All's well that ends well.

Sure, Grant said his mom didn't have much magic, but the government would step in for Reginald Haynes' nephew. They'd have to.

The two bandits were conspiring over Grant's head, discussing the benefits of burner phones over ransom notes.

It was now, or be ransomed right along with Grant.

I dropped to my knees, siphoned a sliver of magic out of the chest, and gave it a whirl.

I want to be able to tell you that I'd never have run out on the kid. But you showed up to this story in good faith, so I'll lay it on the table. If I hadn't caught sight of my invention poking out of the backpack—my very best invention to date —I'm about eighty-five percent sure that I'd have hightailed it up to Kennbire. I'd have felt bad about it, and I might've stopped to phone the cops, but I'd have gone.

Luckily, I did see the invention. I grabbed the mini cannon out of my bag, poured the magic inside, and straightened to find Grant giving me the glare of judgment. He clearly had a sense of what I'd been about to do, but I ignored him and pointed the beautiful, beautiful invention to the sky.

When I told Principal Sanders about letting a phoenix into the file room, it was only half true. I'd actually conjured a phoenix—a living firework—the effect of which was perhaps doubly catastrophic than an actual phoenix would have been, at least when it came to file rooms.

Now, I didn't conjure any old phoenix. No way.

I conjured a dragon.

The emerald green terror descended on the forest with an open jaw, wings spread wide and searing leaves off the branches before pulling a u-ie back toward the treetops, where it circled and prepared to dive again.

As impressed as I was with my own handiwork, I didn't wait to watch the second act. I shoved the magic box into my backpack, grabbed Grant's hand, and pulled him away through the forest while superhero dude and his fair lady Mer screamed bloody murder.

"What the hell was that?" Grant panted. "You captured a dragon in that tube?"

"It'll disappear in thirty to sixty minutes," I said.

"But—"

"Shut up. They'll follow soon." I mixed the last bit of magic in my palm and stirred it up with a whisper, then smeared it into the kid's aura until he disappeared. I did the same for my own aura, and once we were both invisible, we ran like hell.

WE GOT to Ithaca at the ass-crack of dawn. I didn't argue with Grant when he entered Kennbire's address into the GPS on his phone, and we found ourselves outside those impressively warded gates just before sunrise.

We shuffled off our backpacks and sat down on the stone wall, waiting for the school to open. Grant didn't sit on the edge like he had outside Sanders' office. He leaned back on the fence, looking thoroughly dejected. It was disconcerting, to say the least, to see the straight-backed kid affecting my signature slump. I felt like I should go buy him a latte or something, but I had this worm gnawing at my gut like I shouldn't be the first one to speak, even to offer sustenance.

"When were you planning to ditch me?" he asked finally.

"Two days ago."

"Why didn't you?"

"Because you're like a fucking barnacle, man. You didn't give me a chance."

Also, and god help you if you tell Grant Harper this part, but I'm not sure I tried all that hard to get away. Maybe it was OK, for once, to have someone else kicking around with me.

"Why did you trust me, anyway?" I asked. "You knew who I was. I figured you were planning a con of your own."

Grant tucked his hands in his pockets. "I know you're the one who got Tim MacLeod expelled last year when he put Ex Lax in Sanders' coffee."

"Was not."

"Yeah, I saw you climb up the drainpipe to leave the note on her desk. You knew it was his third strike, and you did it anyway."

Whatever. It's not like I deserve a medal for keeping Sanders from getting sick. Tim was the one who cracked under questioning. Like an eggshell.

Grant stared at the tree line, where the lazy-ass sun was trying its best to get out of bed. The clouds were turning pink, so that looked promising. "You should go to Kennbire," he said finally. "I don't know the first thing about magic. You know, my mom tried to tell me magic wasn't real? I believed her until I was seven."

I pictured Grant showing up at elementary school and trying to convince the other kids there was no such thing as magic. Poor kid must have been bullied out of his glasses so many times.

"Kennbire exists to teach you about magic," I said. "You show up with a magical inheritance like that, they won't care if you still don't believe in it. They'll take you. They'll teach you. And hey, you can keep the Study Stick."

"And what about you?" Grant said. "You're just going back to Atchfield?"

I shrugged. "If I'm not expelled."

Grant was still staring at the treetops, like he could will the sun to pop out. Or maybe he wanted to keep it down. Put off that audition meeting a little longer. "Your inventions are pretty good. The dragon especially."

"I can do phoenixes and griffins too."

He nodded, stared at the trees, nodded again. I swear to god, I had no idea what he was thinking until he turned to me with those owl eyes and said, "Sounds like a business that could use a significant investment."

I'd never thought of my little tricks as an ongoing endeavor. I'd never thought of them much at all. A means to an end. A way to waste time. A path, perhaps, to potentially pissing off my father.

The way Grant was looking at me, though, it was almost like he thought I could double his inheritance after all.

And you know what? The kid was right.

RARE

The steak is rare enough to skirt the edge of FDA standards, juices running, tickling your jaw. Your napkin is nowhere to be seen. You eat anyway, without fork or knife, only distantly aware that the waitress is taking her sweet time with that glass of water.

You push the salad away. Lacy arugula tumbles out of the bowl and spills onto the white tablecloth.

No greens, you say. No one hears.

If Kimberly had known restaurants like this existed in the Middle Of Freaking Nowhere, Upstate New York, she might not have protested the move with such vehemence.

Violence, her fiancé would call it. As in, mugs flying into drywall and forfeiting his security deposit in the city, when he told her he'd taken the job without consulting her first.

The presence of a four-star restaurant wouldn't magically transport the ballet to the Catskills, or the Metropolitan Opera, or Bloomingdale's. The fact that it existed here, and without a single pair of antlers on the wall? It was a start.

Kimberly slipped a napkin onto her lap and looked around, appreciating the tasteful paneling and the plastic-but-working greenery draped over the wooden beams. Among the fake leaves, party lights glittered like tiny moons.

She'd describe them that way to Rich, when he arrived. Show him she could say something positive.

When the waitress came over, Kimberly's smile even felt real. "I'll start with water."

You were waiting on someone, but hunger has driven the name from your head. It must be the wine. The world tilts black and white, except for the drops of red on the table-cloth. The hunger is all you know.

You sink your canines into the meat and tear, not caring about the way the other patrons stare, silent. When you glare back, you see that more than one of them has spilled wine. It streams from their mouths in lipstick-red rivulets, the stains blooming across floral print blouses and white button-downs. You don't know how it could have reached your nostrils. The smell of it intoxicates. You want to pad across the room, to suck the wine from the fabric.

You wonder if they will rouse enough to protest.

CHARMING though the place might be, Kimberly's Yelp review would definitely be including a gentle introduction to the concept of a dress code.

Rich would read over her shoulder and call her a snob, but Kimberly couldn't help it. When the group entered the restaurant, it was the only thing she could think.

Five women, all wearing flannel. To *dinner*.

The women arranged themselves in a diamond formation, heels tapping in unison as they followed the hostess across the hardwood floor. At least their footwear was appropriate for fine dining, though they could all have used an introduction to the concept of a pedicure.

Despite the lumberjack fashion statement, they moved with surprising grace. Put them in evening gowns, and they'd look just right on any red carpet.

The tip of the diamond, a woman with straight black hair swinging to her waist—an obvious dye job—stopped at Kimberly's table. Her friends fanned out, arranging themselves into a dizzying semi-circle of denim and plaid, while the hostess hovered a few steps away with her stack of menus, looking confused.

The leader turned catlike eyes to Kimberly.

"Do I know you?" Kimberly asked. She'd met more than a few sorority bitches in her time, but not one of them would have allowed herself to be caught in public without eyeliner.

Kimberly tried not to stare at the blond whose face was marred by a scar that cut from her temple to her jaw. With the right liquid foundation, she ought to be able to cover that right up.

The black-haired woman tilted her sharp chin in the general direction of her friends. "This one."

The scarred one raised a questioning eyebrow, which

only served to emphasize the injury. The alpha merely repeated, "This one," before continuing across the room.

Kimberly watched her walk away, baffled, until something ripped into her neck.

SLOWLY, you realize you are not the only one whose hunger has been sated.

They wait by the door in a diamond formation. By the look of their muzzles, they have been eating rare meat tonight, too.

Their presence should disturb you, though you can't exactly say why.

As the hunger fades, all you want is to join them.

The sleek wolf at the tip of the diamond meets your eyes, a yellow glare.

When you follow, your footprints bleed.

DON'T LOOK BACK

The tabloids say Claude Monty lost his mind over me.

They can't think of another reason the Rock God of the Electric Harp would choose to check himself into a sym home, hook his brain to an artificial reality, and bid the real world farewell. Life might have gone to shit for most of us—hence the stampede to the sym-burbs—but Claude's life still consists of diamond-rimmed cocktails and champagne swimming pools.

They're saying he lost his mind over me.

Maybe they're not wrong.

I can see him from my perch in the sym, calm and still as he waits on the cryo table for the starstruck orderly to put him under. He's removed his hair extensions—of course they're extensions, don't even ask—and stopped taking the dye pills, too. I always wanted him to do that. The gray streaks started in before he turned thirty, so I get why he went with the dyes. But still. I liked the salt among the silky pepper of his hair.

"Is there a way out?" he asks.

Of course he wouldn't have read the whole handbook. Typical Claude.

The orderly practically dives for Claude's chart. "You're checking into...Mr. Monty, you're checking into the Underworld sym. Are you sure—"

"I'm sure," Claude interrupts.

"Because if you want a way out, I could recommend an alternative."

"I'm going to the Underworld. It's where Vi went. It's where I'm going."

Oh boy.

The orderly puts the chart down. "There's no way out of the Underworld, Mr. Monty. It's a permanent decision. Unless you somehow make it to the heart of the game."

Claude picks at his nails, unconcerned.

"Maybe you should try the Magic Moor," the orderly says. He's practically desperate to keep the Harp God awake and functioning on Earth. He might as well start rehearsing the feature story he can sell to the tabloids, because Claude ain't gonna budge. "The Happy Rodent practically leads you to the heart. Or Quest Mountain. Every time you complete a quest, you get a chance to leave."

I want to tell the poor guy not to waste his breath. This is Claude Monty. The world bends to his whims.

Underworld won't.

THE GOV INCHED into our lives like dandelions, at first. Like how you know it's a weed and that it's invasive, ripping health away from the masses to fund cushy seats for elected bottoms—but goddamn if it doesn't vomit pretty flowers every now and then.

Claude condemned the gov in every awards speech, until the gov banned awards.

Like a lot of artists, he got scared. He shut up. And he probably had the least to lose.

Before we knew it, they were in our homes. Watching. We were compelled to watch their nightly propaganda, too, like some *Fahrenheit 451* bullshit. Didn't matter that we all knew what it was, that we'd watched it change.

The borders closed.

Certain websites stopped working, if you didn't know how to bypass a silly little gov-brand censor.

In a corner of Maine, my sister went missing.

It was a small thing. Lots of people went missing, especially in those early days. Some escaped across borders, or found ways to drop off the grid on purpose. But my sister Candace disappeared after a series of cryptic calls and a strange incident with a neighbor peering in the kitchen window—who, when Mom caught her, didn't apologize, but asked if Candace considered herself a patriot.

Claude cried with me, tried to find her even, but he didn't really *get* it. He still had some power in the world, after all. Some pull with the masses. Enough to scare the gov into leaving his family alone.

Not mine, apparently.

The world kept turning. Books showed up on shelves, blondes had more fun on TV, and concerts kept on playing.

My sister never turned up.

You can settle down in a sym world, if you want to. And lots of people do. That's why most of them camp out in the Magic Moor or Quest Mountain. There are roller coasters and evil fill-in-the-blanks to toss into volcanos or lava pits or deep underwater caverns from whence they can resurface ad nauseam. If you go for that kind of thing. But it's optional. Mostly, people are there because when you live in a sym world, you can't get on the bad side of a gov robo-enforcer, or get conscripted into reality TV.

Sym worlds feel safe.

Sym worlds feel like freedom.

That is, until the real world gov decides to pull the plug on the sym homes. It could happen. Claude and I used to talk about that all the time, which is probably why he's here. He doesn't believe I'd make this choice for myself.

He hasn't purchased beach front property on the River Styx, I can tell you that.

I shouldn't have sent him that postcard with the volcano and the cryptic message. Of course he figured it out. It's just, I don't have anyone left. Even after we split, he's the only person left with feet on real ground who actually cares where I might be.

I didn't figure he cared *quite* this much.

Most people who choose the Underworld are looking for a fight. They don't come here unless they can afford to equip their sym selves with swords and spells. Even I'm equipped with Taser rings and poison darts.

The one thing Claude brought with him? His harp.

Seriously, if you're going to a permanent simulated reality, at least give your harp healing properties or a good blasting radius.

But no. Claude's Underworld harp is exactly like his physical one, down to the rubies on the column. He's even had some poor sym specialist design a backpack-slash-amp, so the harp will maintain its electric quality.

That's Claude for you. If it's not a rock harp, it's not worth mentioning.

What he plans to do with that, I can't tell you.

He hasn't bulked up his avatar with the strength of a hundred robo-enforcers or purchased special abilities. He's just Claude Monty, in his skinny jeans and a black turtleneck, carrying a gaudy electric harp through the Underworld.

As one does.

He's the only one on the ferry, chatting it up with Charon.

That's fine. He can make all the friends he wants.

He's not charming his way past Cerberus.

MY INTRODUCTION TO H@DES went something like this.

H@des: youre a tough code wiz to track

Viper_Vi: your message origin has an Underworld sym tag. Since that's not possible, I'm gonna assume you're a scamster. g2go now bye

H@des: no wait

H@des: im writing from underworld. For real

Viper_Vi: not possible

Persephon3: Sure is, honey

Viper_Vi: *furiously tracks source*

Viper_Vi: *stares at screen*

Viper_Vi: *stares at screen*

Viper_Vi: well fuck

Viper_Vi: I can't get you out if that's what you're asking

H@des: want to help us start a revolution?

THAT WAS when shit started to get real. Because don't you know it, I *did* want to start a revolution.

I started shoving my virtual ass through holes in code, while crowbars and plungers got my real-life ass into server farms and safes.

I started breaking down the walls between the syms.

I burst every denial bubble in Ricky-Rodent land, riled up fantasy questers against the real-life enemy. I stirred up some real shit. And when I'd done everything flesh and blood could do, I checked my own body into a sym home. I added myself to the computer system. I slipped that paper nightgown on, and I pulled up the faux wool blanket waiting at the foot of the bed.

When I pricked the IV into my own hand, it stung like a snakebite.

OK. I DIDN'T REALIZE that H@des was such a Claude Monty fan.

For all I know, the guy is an eighty-year-old coin collector. In Underworld, he's got biceps the size of grapefruit, and a pair of hounds that flank his every step. He towers over everyone, both physically and intellectually.

Or so I thought.

The guy took one look at Claude and lost his shit.

"Claude fucking Monty showed up in my sym," he says. He's practically dancing in a circle, which looks ridiculous on his bare-chested avatar. He's flipped the Pits of Surveillance to show Claude and only Claude, so everything that's happening elsewhere in the Underworld—and what

we can see of the outer world which, thanks to me, is a lot—
has gone silent. Not a good call, H@des. Who knows what
Furies_3 will get up to without us keeping watch?

H@des doesn't care. "Do you think he'll autograph my
sword?"

"No," I say, "because he'll never get this far."

"Come on, Viper_Vi," he says, "help him."

"No way."

He turns to me, and for a second I get what Persephon3
sees in him. He's convincing. That's why we're primed to
strike. "Think about it, Vi," he says. "Claude Monty. On our
side. It's huge."

H@des has to know Claude's my ex. "He won't help us,
man," I say.

"You can convince him."

I couldn't convince him to keep looking for Candace. He
gave up, the same way he'd walk away from a long line in a
coffee shop. He could've used his influence; he didn't.

How am I going to convince him to start a revolution?

But Claude Monty is here. Now. He's not sitting in a
hotel room with eyes puffed from crying, or strumming
dolefully on his harp like that's going to stop me from pack-
ing. He took action. He's *here*.

"Underworld is your dominion," I tell him. "You do it."

"Underworld is my dominion. Claude Monty is yours."

The Underworld King hath spoken. I sigh and start
changing settings like the genius I am, and poof, alakazam,
now Cerberus is coded to cave to any Claude Monty song.

Of course Claude knows he's supposed to croon the dog
to sleep, though previously the only tune that would give
the puppy a night-night was "Catch a Falling Star." Now,
Claude strums his harp, his hair rocking in silken waves as
he moves, and I recognize the opening strain of his first hit,

"Harp-Way to the Sun," before the slobbering monster drops his heads on his paws and starts to snooze.

That thing is just a bundle of binary, but it's still gross.

Of course I fucking recognized Claude Monty when I first laid eyes on him. I recognized him and I cursed him out, obviously, for not throwing a tip into the jar at the coffee shop when he was Claude fucking Monty.

It turned out he'd tipped via his app, and that he'd tipped triple what he paid for his latte. I asked him what other sins he'd committed recently. He claimed overdue library books, so I reamed him out for that one, and we were laughing by the end of it.

He ended up asking me to dinner. And I ended up accepting, because who doesn't like a guy who gets turned on by a public scolding?

The day I fell in love with Claude was the day he asked me what I'd do, what I'd want to see, if I could live in a pre-gov world. We were tangled together on his too-comfortable leather couch, his phone blinking with a weekend's worth of ignored calls from his manager, and the question came out of nowhere.

The right answer, the Miss America answer, would've been one of those kill-the-dictator conundrums, an unanswerable series of "what ifs" that I'd have attempted if he'd asked me after Candace went missing.

Instead, I went with the whimsical.

"Snow," I said. "If I could go back, I'd want to play in the snow."

H@des is as transfixed by Claude's song as his pooch. And because I've been here more than thirty seconds, I anticipate his next move: he snaps his fingers, and suddenly Claude is standing next to us in the control room.

Always a fun trick.

"Let her go," Claude says, giving me the opportunity to note that bravery looks wrong on him. Like an oversized coat—though I have to admit it's one he might grow into someday, if he tries.

H@des is pretty fanned out, staring at Claude like he's never seen anything so beautiful in his life, which I'm thinking Persephon3 would probably resent.

"Vi is essential to our operation," H@des says.

"Let her go," Claude repeats. Eloquent.

H@des is pacing, which means he's got a plan. I wish I could hack his brain to see what it is. "That song you played out there was pretty damn beautiful," he says. "You play that for the people locked in the syms, you'd bring them over to our side in droves."

"I'm not a pied piper, and I'm not here for a revolution," Claude says. "I'm here for Vi."

"Play," H@des commands.

Claude is not used to being commanded.

But the tabloids say Claude Monty lost his mind over me, and I guess he has. He picks up his harp, and I can see he spared no expense on his avatar; its range of emotions wide enough to send teenage audiences into fits of desire. He's looking at his harp like it's his salvation.

Maybe it is.

He plucks the opening riff, a melody that ought to sound rinky-dink but somehow transcends its simplicity. I must've heard it a thousand times, ringing through stadium concerts, stopping conversations at parties, and, later, bouncing tinnily out of my car speakers before I could switch the station. I've heard it so many times, and still I'm only half immune.

H@des, though, is a goner. The Underworld King is frozen as he watches Claude's pixel-fingers caress the harp. It's not easy to stop H@des in his tracks like that; he might seem like a cozy kind of eccentric, but he's the leader of a revolution.

He'll write a code to murder you before he'll let you betray him, and he won't be sorry about it. He'll shut down whole sym worlds—bad news for the inhabitants—before he'll let the gov win.

But Claude could've had a career in hypnotism. Too bad it's not quite as snazzy as the rock-harp-star life.

He finishes his song. Too soon. Too late.

"All right," H@des says. His voice sounds rough, almost grating after the lullaby of Claude's spell. "You can take her out."

I squeak in protest as Claude stands. H@des holds up a hand. "On one condition."

Claude sits.

"You can take her out," H@des says, "if you turn and walk out this door, and never once look behind you. If you check for her, if you so much as glance over your shoulder, I'll throw you out of Underworld. You'll never see it again."

I wouldn't mind committing a couple of murders myself right now, the way these two showboats are talking about me like I'm not even here. "Do I get a say in this?" I ask.

Claude doesn't look my way; I wonder if he can hear me.

H@des just shakes his head. Nope.

"I should get a say in this," I say. "You need me."

When I catch my reflection in the surveillance monitor, I

can see why Claude is ignoring me. I'm nothing more than a shadow; a wisp of a ghost.

The Underworld is H@des' dominion.

"What's the catch?" Claude asks.

"No catch," H@des says.

Claude shoulders his harp, eyes searching the room behind H@des. His gaze glances off me, twice. I want to jump up and down and scream at the top of my lungs, but it won't do me any good. "How will I know she's there?" Claude asks.

"You won't."

"It sounds too easy."

H@des smiles, and it's not a pretty one. "No magical teleporting this time," he says. "This time, you follow the maze."

THE MAZE IS A LIE.

In truth, the maze is a black tunnel that burrows straight under Cerberus, under the Styx, all the way to the lava-red EXIT sign. Claude could follow it straight back to his comfy sym home and startle the fuck out of that tsking orderly.

But the tunnel is called the maze, because that's the kind of douchebag H@des can be, and Claude hesitates. He's looking for the first fork, or listening for my footsteps, or second guessing his choice. I don't know.

If he looks back, I'll hate his weakness.

If he doesn't, I'll hate his resolve.

No matter what happens, I'll never belong to Claude Monty again.

I belong to the syms, until the revolution drills a hole through these virtual walls and storms the real world. H@des knows it. Claude should know it, too.

After what feels like a lifetime of indecision, Claude forges ahead. No sign of weakening. I'm still a shadow, my ghostly form tethered to Claude's footsteps as if by an invisible cord.

My play can be just as vicious as H@des'. My sym knowledge is nearly as vast.

I start by making it snow.

It shouldn't be possible. The tunnel is hot as—well, not to be cliche, but you know—but I thrive on the impossible. I *am* the impossible.

Claude stops. Catches a snowflake on his finger. He knows what snow means to me. He knows what I'd do to get it. "Vi?"

"Set me free," I say.

The snowflake melts. He can't hear me.

I let him take a few more steps,

I build trees. I am imagining this place even more than I imagined the snow, constructing it out of dreams. The walls that loom ahead surround the fortress of my worst nightmares, the sight that woke me screaming in his arms more times than I care to remember.

I steel my heart, and I build the prison. I weave weeping through the simmering whispers of the trees. I add a rancid smell.

H@des does not stop me.

At Claude's feet, I build a path.

He stares at it, breathing hard. He repeats my name.

This time, I don't bother to answer. He knows I'm here; that's not what this is about. I'm trusting him to decipher the message I'm sending through the sym.

I'm trusting him to honor it.

Claude adjusts his harp, a tic he never demonstrated in real life, and tiptoes down the path.

I let him reach the gate before I let my sister out.

She leads a tangled group of captives, a jumble of ragged clothing and shoeless feet. I make myself collapse her cheeks to gauntness and grease her hair into strings. I wilt her skin around gangly bones and give her the wide-eyed horror I feel every time I see her this way.

Claude knows her. It might be shame that hunches his shoulders. It might be pain.

It might be acceptance.

"You want to stay," he says.

I allow the nightmare to fade.

Claude watches the images disappear, like he's searing the memory into his mind. I wonder if he'll write a song about this. I wonder if I'd mind.

When Candace's ghost is gone, Claude turns to face mine.

Our eyes meet. I pop him a salute. He surprises me by popping one right back.

Somewhere in the Underworld, H@des snaps his fingers, and I dissolve.

~

With H@des' rhetoric and my know-how, we're gonna stage a fucking coup. Their phones will die. Their in-home assistants will falter. Their fitness watches will stop tracking their every move.

We'll control it all.

And we're doing it from inside the sym.

The Underworld is coming up. Until it does, Viper_Vi is staying down.

~

INSUBSTANTIAL

Calliope cannot convince her blood to circulate.

It is the sensation of waking with one arm splayed on the pillow, the limb drained and temporarily useless—only it tingles throughout her body. She can't convince her numb fingers to grasp the doorknob.

The window is open, and she sneaks onto the slope of the roof more easily than ever before. Though she can't manage her usual grip on the gutter, her ankles don't smart when she lands.

She is weightless. She almost giggles, thinking of how she will surprise her mother by walking in the front door. But a cold feeling against her spine stifles her laughter. It is like getting up to use the bathroom at night, when the darkness convinces her to waste no time in returning to her room, lest the monsters should realize there's a morsel out of bed.

If she loses her grip on the earth she will fly away, a balloon without a tether.

Calliope gives her head a shake, willing the dizziness to pass. Soon she will go inside, where her mother will press a cool hand against her forehead and check for fever. For now, she scans the yard for something familiar. The trees tilt, and she blinks to set them right. The flowerbeds wobble from daffodil to snapdragon, a double exposure in her brain.

Through the chaos, she catches sight of her lunchbox, anchored in the grass. She tries to remember the last time she held the handle, but it's hard to distinguish the difference between days and years.

It should not be here. It belongs on the kitchen counter, jaw unhinged, waiting to be sated with peanut butter sandwiches and notes from her mother: *Don't forget to hand in your lunch money!* Always with a heart.

On the street, kids hurry by, backpacks quivering as they cast wide-eyed glances at the house. Calliope kneels before the lunchbox. She expects damp knees, but no sensation leaks through her jeans.

There are two boys beyond the fence now, poking noses and fingers between the bars and whispering, jabbing one another with elbows. Calliope cannot hear what they're saying. She wants them to leave her alone.

The lunchbox is decorated with a unicorn. There are rainbows on the thermos. But the hinges are rusty, the unicorn's horn all but faded away.

Calliope reaches for the clasp.

One of the boys squeezes between the bars of the fence, pauses, looks back to his friend. The friend urges him on with a bright red sleeve.

"What do you want?" asks Calliope. The boy looks past her and swallows, then darts toward the porch.

Calliope decides to pay him no mind. She touches the tip of her index finger to the clasp on the unicorn lunchbox.

Her finger disappears. When she pushes forward, alarmed, the rest of her hand follows.

She jerks it back.

The boy reaches the porch, touches the bottom step. For a moment, the house settles in Calliope's vision, and she sees it as if for the first time.

The porch swing hangs drunkenly from one chain. The welcome mat is gone. The kitchen window is broken, mold-black curtains hanging dirty and frayed.

It's disorienting, like stumbling into a carnival and searching for a familiar strain through the cacophony of clashing tunes.

The boy hurtles back down the walk while his companion giggles.

Calliope is heat. She pours it into her fingers, curls them around the handle, and hurls the lunchbox with all the substance she has left.

The boys scream when the box hits the fence. They run.

Calliope sinks once more to her knees and tries to piece it all together, her thoughts no more solid than the ground beneath her feet. She will grow too heavy for the surface and descend through layers of earth, forget her place in time and fall through the years, until everything exists at once. She will hear the reason for the cockroaches, and how they keep the melody of the world from tilting off key.

The day slinks on.

～

CALLIOPE CANNOT CONVINCE her blood to circulate.

～

INTERPLANETARY GHOST RUSHERS

I'm sorry to say that by the time my parents joined the Interplanetary Ghost Rush and yanked us off to Planet 14, the only spirits left there were rumors.

At least there's still a tourist industry.

Well. I should clarify that.

Say you're on your way to ski on Planet 16, or to meet Astro Mickey Mouse on Planet 21. So you stop on the way to refuel your space porter, maybe stock the snack bin with fresh moon fries. And where do you get those moon fries?

That would be Planet 14. The pit stop of planets.

Best bathrooms in the galaxy.

But on the way to the surface, your porter might hit a block of ice, because flying ice loves P-14 more than a black hole loves matter. So you might end up with a ruptured solar panel or leaky fuel tank. And if *that* happens, you *might* decide to kill time with a visit to the Planet 14 Ghost Mining Museum (P14GMM) to kill time while your porter gets repaired.

Or you might stick around the mechanic's waiting room all day drinking bad coffee and watching reruns of *Who*

Wants to be a Cosmic Millionaire. The entertainment value is about equal.

Luckily, someone's gotta hawk key fobs to the five visitors who wander in every week. So while my parents dig fruitlessly for ghost energy, I've got a job in the P14GMM gift shop.

My boss, Mr. Difrizplfkjdmnophodole, isn't human. It's not an insult. It's a fact. He's one of the aliens that've shared P-14 with humans since the alliance of 3800.

We humans don't have enough throats to pronounce the aliens' proper name, so we call them Rocklings because they hail from the Asteroid belt between Planets 4 and 5.

I'm thinking Mr. D's museum-slash-keychain-stand is probably some kind of a front. Slot machines in the basement, maybe. But I basically get paid to sit behind a counter playing games on my handheld and talking to my friends back on P-1 (when I've got enough credits for inter-planet communication, which at the moment, I don't).

I'm not about to ask any questions.

This morning, I'm so occupied with plans for obliterating space noodles with my thumbs until my paycheck comes in, I don't see the new girl until I'm almost sitting on her.

"Excuse me," she says, in this prim little voice—like my very breathing might upset her stomach. "This area is for employees only."

"I *am* an employee," I say. "I'm Maddie."

"Oh," she says, dismissive. She's a Rockling like Mr. D, her arms willowy and elbow-less, which I can see because she's wearing a purple tube top. Just looking at her makes me shiver; I'm wearing three sweatshirts, a scarf, and a knitted cap. The Rockling girl's ears are like giant saucers, giving her this kitten level of cuteness that's immediately annoying.

"Uncle D didn't say there'd be another girl," she says.

For a second, I wonder if Mr. D found the words I spelled with the personalized key chains last week.

Maybe I'm fired.

But then she says, "I'm Rose. I was bored, so I asked to work here today."

I laugh. It sounds loud and rude next to her musical voice. "You think working here will make you less bored?"

She folds her hands in her lap. "I'm all for new experiences."

"Yeah, OK. Well, I'm all for a paycheck. So let me behind the counter, please."

"You don't look old enough to work here."

"I'm going into seventh grade," I say, indignant. Of course, everyone else on this planet is chasing ghosts, selling fuel, or fixing porters, so I'm pretty much Mr. D's only option.

She doesn't need to know that.

Rose glances at the ceiling. It's not an "I'm-considering-your-request" glance. It's an "I-hid-my-poker-winnings-up-there" glance, which I've seen any number of times after my older brother comes back from a spin on lucky Planet 7.

But Rose must decide she doesn't want me asking questions. She relents.

There's only one stool, though, and she's perched on it with her knees curled beneath her, skirt puffing out like a colorful mushroom.

Rocklings do better in the P-14 cold than humans do.

I prop my handheld on the counter and get to work blasting space noodles. Usually, I try to make my communication credits stretch the full two weeks between paychecks.

But Aly's cat died last week, so I spent everything in the first three days, cheering her up in conference chats with our other friend, Tina.

I miss them so much it aches.

They're going to start seventh without me.

"Excuse me," Rose says, as I blast rotini out of orbit with my meatball lasers.

I look at her, confused.

She points at the handheld. Her hands are too clean. Because the A-belt is sooo much more civilized than P-14.

"Your sound effects," she says. "They're interfering."

"With what?" I ask. "Your staring?"

"No. My listening."

I listen.

Silence.

I raise my eyebrows—I've been working on that one-at-a-time thing, which would come in really useful at moments like this—and cup my ears, exaggerating.

I'm not expecting to hear a thing.

Above us, something crashes to the floor, shaking the whole ceiling. "Oh, right," I say. "Don't worry. Gus knocks over the Phantoms of Pluto display every day around this time. He's right on schedule."

Always denies it, too. Like I care that he's clumsy.

Rose's eyes are on the ceiling, like those poker winnings are in danger.

"I'll go check," I say.

I wish I could tell you I'm offering because I'm nice and want to comfort her. But I just kind of want to know what her deal is.

Rose slips down from the stool and brushes past me. "I'll check."

I shrug. Fine.

My astro-cats have fettuccini to destroy.

IN ADDITION to walls and warmth and people to talk to, what I really miss about P-1 is my gerbil, Ginger. I hope Aly's taking good care of her, and letting her run in her ball.

I just got paid. I can ask Aly myself. Maybe even splurge on a few minutes of video. I always transfer most of my credits to Mom, to help out with the household budget (or tent-hold budget, since the home my parents snagged us here is literally a canvas dome). But she's firm about me keeping a few credits for myself.

Ginger would not have loved P-14, or the not-so-super dome where we live. It's not a whole lot warmer than the outside—where I swear there are ice crystals collecting between my fingers. And there's not much privacy. Which, I guess, is not such a big deal for a gerbil. But before I even open the door, I can hear Mom and Dad talking about how many ghosts they snagged this week.

None. It's always none.

Ghosts are residual energy. That's it. They wander around, looking all human, but the souls that inhabited them are gone. They don't talk. They don't avenge wrongs. They don't try to finish any business. They're just energy, trapped in old patterns.

When you suck up that energy with kinetically modified fiberglass tubing, you can sell the capsule for a couple thousand credits.

Which is why Mom and Dad dragged me out to the boonies of the solar system after my brother pulled his own energy miracle and ghosted with their life savings. He's probably tossed it onto a roulette wheel by now.

"We can scrape by this week if we skip coffee," Mom says. They're calculating numbers on Dad's handheld. The screen busted last week when it took a tumble from his bunk to the floor, which is basically a tarp laid over ice. The poor thing never had a chance.

He doesn't say anything. I know without looking that he's scanning the numbers, trying to figure out how Mom can have coffee while we all still consume actual calories.

"It was supposed to be easier here," Mom says.

We were never supposed to be here at all.

When I finally get the guts to open the door, I take dinner to my bunk in the corner, and I transfer my entire paycheck, measly as it is, from my account to Mom's.

At the very least, she should get her coffee.

MOM DOESN'T SAY anything about the credits over breakfast, but she gives my arm an extra squeeze as I head out the door-slash-tent-flap.

In all the excitement of not being like my jerk of a brother, I forget about Rose until my hand's on the museum door.

Maybe she won't be here today. Maybe it'll just be me and the space noodles. My goal is to have them all completely Bolognese-d by the time I can talk to Aly again.

I pass the Early Ghost Catching display—as if the discovery of Martian spirit energy a thousand years ago is anything more than a boring history lesson—as quickly as I can. This place couldn't possibly have been enough to satisfy her boredom.

But she's back on my stool, wearing an orange headband to hold back her metallic silver locks, and a matching tank top. There's no way it's so cold in the A-belt that she's comfortable in that.

She's got her eyes rolled toward the ceiling, in a move my brother would call "giving away your hand." I let the door clatter to a close, making Rose jump. Which is how I know she's not faking.

I'm forming a plan to propose a museum exploration, just so I can figure out what she's up to, when Mr. D himself lopes in. I'm pretty sure he bought this old fort for the high ceilings, even though his ears come close to brushing them.

He clears his throats. "Business isn't booming," he says, and pauses. Like we need a few moments to digest that news flash. "I need more postcards delivered to mechanic's row, and the fueling stations. And anywhere else you can think of."

"Mr. D," I say, trying to be gentle, "the last time I brought cards around, I got yelled at for talking over a Space Jeopardy answer."

It was 'What is Astronaut Ice Cream,' which they should have known anyway.

"Wait for a commercial break." He snaps his fingers, ears quivering. "*You* be the commercial, Maddie."

It'll be a real shame if it turns out Mr. D doesn't actually have slot machines in the back. If I lose this job, I'm not sure my family will eat at all. But the way he's looking at me, he really wants this place to work out.

He's a historian. Not a criminal.

We're in trouble.

Mr. D's shaking the cards at me. "Come on, Maddie. I got a tip about a deal on antique energy lasers on Moon 7. If that won't bring in some curious customers, well, I don't know what will."

Something interesting, maybe. Like holos depicting real

ghosts, or interactive enhanced-reality displays, or a range where visitors can try out actual Ecto-hoses.

OK, that last one is unlikely. But you get the idea.

"I'm heading out there for a day or two," he adds. "I need these postcards distributed in the meantime."

"I'll do it, Uncle D," Rose says, before I can agree. I shouldn't be surprised that she's sweet as her name when a grownup's around.

Mr. D grins and hands her the cards.

I can't believe she's willing to leave the museum, and her secret.

In fact, I don't believe it. So as soon as Mr. D's gone, I follow his niece out of the gift shop.

IT FEELS SO good to be right.

Rose doesn't leave the museum. Instead, she loops around and skips up the narrow staircase in back.

This place used to be a fort. Fifty years ago, humans and Rocklings thought there might be a fight over P-14, until they all sat down together and figured they could share.

Before that, though, the humans used this spot as a military base. And before *that*, it was the site of the first P-14 colony.

This is the kind of useless knowledge you acquire when you work in a museum.

Rose takes the staircase from the courtyard where the soldiers used to do their exercises, and goes all the way up to the old barracks. I follow at a distance, careful to mind the creaky screws on the step between the third and fourth floors.

When I hear her voice, I stop.

"...left Chewy in the A-belt with Mom and Dad," she's saying. "They said it's too cold here for a dog, but they're wrong. The A-belt is way colder."

Rose is missing a pet she left in the A-belt? Is she hiding a stray dog up here?

I'd hide a stray gerbil, if I could.

I peer around the corner.

When I see who Rose is talking to, I can barely retrain a squeak of surprise. In the middle of the floor is a boy about our age, maybe twelve or thirteen, and he's tossing something to the end of the hall in an eight-second loop.

The boy is a ghost.

And my family's problems are solved.

IT'S NOT hard to nick Mom's Ecto-hose for a night of ghost hunting. The not-so-super dome has no closets or hooks, so she coils the hose into a careful heap by the door when she comes home.

Sneaking out is a little more nerve wracking. But Mom and Dad work so hard all day, picking up odd jobs where ghosts are scarce—which they always are—so once they're asleep, they're dead to the planet. I manage not to knock over any chairs, and make it outside without waking them.

P-14 is weird at night. Frost crunches under my boots, and the whole dome-village where we live is silent. There are a few spots of glowing lamps, people and Rocklings awake here and there, but they're easy enough to avoid.

The Planet 14 Ghost Mining Museum isn't as weird. Here, I'm used to the silence.

I sneak in the back, heading up the stairs.

The boy with the invisible dog probably doesn't come

out at night. The ghosts all have their cycles, their times. But if the boy is still here, I'm sure the Planet 14 Ghost Mining Museum hasn't been swept for ghosts at all.

Ironic.

It's not the kind of thing Mr. D would think to have done. He spends most of his time staring at books about ghosts. I can definitely see him missing real ones. I should have thought of it, though. Gus knocking over that display every day at the same time and denying it? That reeks of ghost activity.

I don't have to wait long before I find more.

Or rather, it finds me: the sound of marching, invading my stairwell in a sudden wash of rhythm.

I peek onto the second floor.

It's three pairs of feet, attached to three human ghost soldiers. They look young. They look scared.

If anything makes sense to me, it's that. They're soldiers reviewing their exercises in the dead of night, on a planet where they might be obliterated. They repeated this action so much, and with such intensity, that a bit of their energy returned here after their deaths.

They must have been terrified.

Well, so am I. I tug the Ecto-hose loose from my backpack and creep forward.

As soon as the ghosts march back to my end of the room, they'll be porter fuel, and Mom can have all the coffee she wants.

I make my move.

Someone tackles me from behind, arms latching behind my knees. I scream as my attacker falls with me, shoving my cheek against the cold linoleum.

When I scramble around, it's Rose who's trying to avoid getting kicked in the face.

"What the Jupiter?!" I say as the ghosts march over us, sending thrills of static electricity through my limbs. It's eerie and invigorating, and super creepy.

"They're my friends," Rose sobs. "You can't."

"It's just energy. The people are long gone."

I really want to move out of their way, though. They're tingly.

She's too busy crying to answer. I think of her dog back in the A-belt, and I realize I don't know anything about her. Why she's here. Where her parents might be, if Mr. D is her uncle.

How she developed killer tackling skills.

My hands are smushed behind me, and Rose is gripping my knees like she's got her own gravity. Tears track down her face, and her silver hair is wild around her head.

"OK," I say. "OK. Let's talk."

THE SOLDIERS and the boy are only a beginning. There's a woman in an empty room upstairs, opening invisible drawers as she searches for something she's lost. There's a captain talking into his comm and writing notes, late into the P-14 night.

We go back to the soldiers when I've seen the rest, to watch them pace. They screw up their formation, try again. March out of step, try again. Endlessly.

"You talk to them?" I ask. It doesn't seem likely; they ignore us, like holos in an enhanced reality program. If we could ask them, they'd be afraid of Rose; they'd think she and the Rocklings want to kill them.

Rose passes through the middle soldier to plop cross-legged in the corner, saucer ears drooping.

I wait for them to march by before joining her.

"All my friends are on A-7471," she says.

"And your dog."

She's not surprised I know about him. "And Chewy. Yeah. We don't...there aren't any ghosts in the A-belt. I've never heard of a non-human ghost at all. I really wanted to see one. So I came here and explored the museum, and I found a bunch."

Enough to feed a family of three until I'm old enough to get a real job.

Rose seems to know what I'm thinking. "You can't mine them, Maddie. They're safe here."

I want to repeat that it's just energy. There've been a gazillion tests to prove it. Atmospheric pressure readings and radar screenings and pass after pass with the best séance technology on the market.

But right now, I see three nervous ghosts running drills, again and again. Afraid.

They don't know the Rocklings will turn out to be our friends.

They don't know it's the other humans that might not be, that we'll show up to wrench the last shreds of them into capsules for space porters.

I sit back against the wall and bounce my head against my ponytail bump.

And I tell Rose everything. My brother's gambling and my parents' attempts to help, their debt, his disappearance. Our last house on P-1 and the ball course we made for Ginger.

"They brought us here for a fresh start," I finish.

Quick money. Quick fix. It never works that way.

The end of the story is hanging. Rose knows how few ghosts there are left to mine out here.

"Uncle D came for the same reasons, I guess," she sighs. "My parents sent me here to 'help' during the school break. While they 'figure out' their relationship."

Translation: while they decide whether to stay together. I get it.

"Seems no one can make money on P-14," she adds.

That makes me sit up. I look at her. "I hadn't seen ghosts before I came to P-14, either."

"They haven't figured out how to find them on P-1 yet."

It's kind of the whole point. Why their energy was never mined before. Some atmospheres won't show them, or won't hold them. No one knows.

"This place has a built-in audience," I continue. "We just need the right hook."

No one wants to look at glorified posters, or stand and read Mr. D's dry stories about pre-ghost energy or the eighty-eight parts of an Ecto-hose (and how to clean it).

But they might want to see *real* ghosts.

I think I know how to save both our families.

GETTING the word out is easy. I borrow a couple credits from Rose so I can ping the details to Aly, and I ask her to pass it on.

Which she does. Because the idea is so cool it'd thrive on P-14 like a polar bear, that's why.

Rose sends it to her friends, too, and by the time Mr. D gets back from Moon 7, our ad's gone viral. He's just standing there, jaw ajar, as he stares at the crowd in front of his museum. He can't even take a step without someone telling him to wait his turn.

Rose and I are selling admission tickets as fast as we can,

and she's announcing that, "The lonely wanderer emerges from the attic in approximately five minutes. If you have tickets, please make your way to the stairs."

"This viewing is sold out," I add, as people and Rocklings jostle closer. P-14's economy just got the boost of a lifetime. "But a game of tag will knock over the Pluto display upstairs in half a spin, and we've got a chicken crossing the coop in ten. Those are included in general admission."

We don't know why the chicken shows up and the dog doesn't.

Ghost energy still has its mysteries.

"What is going on here?" Mr. D calls, when he gets his vocal cords working. He's still stuck in the doorway.

"We added a few exhibits," Rose says. "You don't mind Uncle D, do you?"

I can practically see credit tokens flashing in his eyes. Imagine how many history books he can buy with them. Bricks and bricks. "I think I'm going to need a bigger staff," he says.

We'd counted on that.

Mom and Dad are already clipping tickets in the courtyard.

"Maybe Planet 14 is more than just a pit stop, after all," Rose says.

Maybe she's right. Maybe I've got a new friend.

Next mission: convincing Mr. D to add sweatshirts to the gift shop.

MBEDI

No one wants a cake for their sixteenth birthday, or a car, or a bouquet of drone balloons that can deliver pizzas and spy on the neighbors.

All anyone wants for any birthday is a new mBedi, which is why I'm sitting at the table with my arms crossed while Mom shakes sprinkles onto a chocolate cake she made herself.

It's like we're part of the Venus colony or something. They might have a reason to go basic. We don't.

Mom lights candles by swiping a wooden stick across the side of a box—which, by the way, would be unnecessary if she had a starter switch installed between her thumb and index finger like normal people—and looks at me proudly, as if I'm supposed to be impressed at her dexterity with ancient technology.

"Go ahead," she says. "Blow them out."

Two years until I'm old enough to authorize my own mBedis. Two years.

I give a half-hearted puff. One of the candles flickers.

"Come on, Laurel, with gusto," she says. "Get it? GUST-o.

Like a gust of wind. Like you mean it."

"I get it," I mutter. "And I don't mean it."

Mom's face clouds over. "Well then, I think I'll wish for an mBedi to magically appear on your butt cheek."

"Better than nothing."

Mom blows out the candles. "You've got what you need."

Not really, no. I've got the required messaging mBedi installed on the back of my left hand, maps on the palm. Other kids have games, readers, search tools, calorie counters. One girl can change the color of her eyes with a tap to the temple. My friend Martha can do the same to her hair. Every time I go out with my friends, one of them has to place the order for me on her restaurant mBedi so I won't be the freak standing in line clutching paper currency.

It's as if Mom time traveled here from an era when people carried plastic credit cards instead of scanning a barcode in their pinky fingers.

"Picture yourself at eighty years old with Peppermint Smash Mountain permanently installed on your thigh," Mom says. "Will you love it then?"

"I'll run updates. Replace it."

"A fad is a fad," Mom says. She cuts herself a big piece of cake and starts eating.

She doesn't offer me a slice.

I endure my pathetic birthday celebration for as long as I can before excusing myself under the guise of wanting to see my friends.

Instead, I go to the mBedi store.

The walls are made of see-through touch screens, a cube of building-sized mBedis in the middle of the city. They're billboards, basically, and the courtyard around the store is one big ad. As you walk up, squares that looked like regular concrete come to life beneath your feet. A girl with a huge smile demonstrates self-cleaning dental mBedis. A boy invites you to try the new inner-eyelid virtual reality mBedis, which have got to be painful to install.

Usually I walk around and try all the blocks in the ground because I'm too shy to go up to the walls. Sixteen years old and I can't even go into the store that everyone else treats like an extension of home.

But today I feel reckless.

There's a wait for the wall, but I don't mind. I stand behind a pair of tween queens—Mom would call them "teenie boppers"—with feathery pink hair ties and mBedis glowing on their arms, though I can't see what kind. They're waiting to try a Hovertile, which only works on closed courses and requires a license you can't get until you turn fifteen. The tween queens might be getting ahead of themselves.

They step onto the tile together—it looks like any other mBedi tile, part of the digital mosaic of the mBedi store only it works together with the wall—and one of them presses the start button.

"I'm sorry," the wall tells them in a pleasant female voice. "Your age chip indicates you are not authorized to operate this mBedi. Please return in two-point-one years, Lila, and one-point-seven years, Wendy."

"It won't even let us try?" says either Lila or Wendy. "It's not like we're going to crash a stupid display model."

"So dull," says the other, and they turn away to head for the next wall.

I step forward. "Wait," I say. "Get behind me for a sec."

They exchange a glance. I know they must be noting my lack of mBedis, and the fact that I'm here by myself. Talk about dull. But after a second, Lila and Wendy slip between my back and the people who wait impatiently behind me.

"Authorized, Laurel," the voice says. "Happy birthday. Please stand on the glass tile with your feet planted shoulder-width apart. Hovering initiating in three, two—"

"OK," I tell the girls, "hop on."

"—one."

The glass tile rises, and I jump off—staying exactly in front of the mBedi screen—as the girls leap up. The system allows me to control it for a few more seconds on the glass, pushing the girls up farther, then sideways in the small cube allowed by the trial. I can't help thinking how cool it would be to ride one of these things on a Hovertile team, zooming around obstacles while the crowd cheers. They're already talking about making it an Olympic event.

The girls giggle uncontrollably and clutch at each other until the wall says, "Unauthorized riders. Goodbye."

The wall shuts down, and the glass tile delivers Lila and Wendy safely to the ground.

"Thanks," one of them says, and they run off.

Before I step aside to give the next shoppers their shot, I glance inside the store. Just for a second, because it's not like I get this close very often. Or ever. Behind the translucent images of the rebooting wall, I catch the eye of a girl who's standing inside, watching me. She's about my age, with dyed black hair tucked behind her ears, and she's wearing the blue shirt and lanyard that indicate her as an mBedi store employee. Before she can call me out for breaking the rules, I spin around and hurry toward home.

MOM's ATTITUDE is icy for a few days after my birthday, which I actually kind of enjoy. Life without lectures? Sign me up.

She's too cheerful to keep it up, though, so it's less than a week before she's suggesting a movie marathon with popcorn she made on the stove.

"I'm supposed to meet Jane and Martha," I say.

Mom waves the bowl of popcorn and winks. "More for me," she says, and drifts into the living room, where she has an old-fashioned flat screen mounted on the wall for watching movies.

This is why I can't have people over.

I'M early to meet my friends, so I haunt the mBedi store until the sales girl who was watching me on my birthday comes outside with a spray bottle and a soft cloth. But instead of washing the display mBedis, she stalks over to me, shoulders hunched, and looks me over like I'm something she found in her shoe. She's a few inches shorter than me, and she doesn't seem to think staring is rude. The plastic tag on her shoulder says Val.

"You could use an upgrade," she says, and even though it's true I'm not sure if I like her for saying it.

"You probably work on commission," I say, and I manage not to cringe even though it's exactly what Mom would say.

"Is money the problem, or is it your parents?"

"Parents. I mean, Mom."

"Then I can get you an mBedi," she says. "Whatever kind you want."

I narrow my eyes, resisting the urge to mimic her rounded posture. "How?"

She blinks. On anyone else, I think, it would be a full-on eye roll. "Meet me here at seven, and make sure you know what you want."

Before I can ask more questions, she slumps away, spray bottle in hand, and disappears inside without cleaning a single tile.

Any mBedi Val can get me without Mom's permission is going to be against the rules. Only the mBedi store is authorized to install, so either she's talking about stolen mBedis—which I'm not sure I can get behind, even though the mBedi store practically owns the world right now—or she's talking about unauthorized installation. Maybe both.

Either way, I know I shouldn't do it. I head to the coffee shop to meet Martha and Jane, feeling like a coward.

It's even worse when I see them. I walk into the coffee shop, and they've both got their t-shirts rolled up, staring at each other's stomachs. I'm trying to think of some quip I can make about stripping in public when I see they're analyzing each other's fancy new screens.

"What's this?" I ask, sticking my head down beside Martha's pink-streaked one, which is about an inch from Jane's stomach. They're both so startled that they jump, then start giggling. Jane's stomach mBedi gives off a wild punctuation of hot pink fireworks, beautiful against her dark complexion.

"They're mood mBedis," Jane says as Martha straightens. "We ordered you a coffee. Milk, no sugar."

We've known each other since kindergarten. We used to call ourselves the triplets because we're all about the same height, even though we don't look alike in any other way. Martha's got blond hair, currently with pink highlights, Jane's hair is black and curly, and mine falls into the mousy-brown category. The whole triplet thing fell away when they started to get matching mBedis in middle school, but they've never been awful enough to start saying they're twins. We're still close, I guess.

"A mood mBedi?" I ask, because I'm in danger of not getting filled in now that the colors are cooling into pools of blue and green, their excitement apparently waning.

The center of the cafe table opens, and a tray rises to deliver our drinks. My coffee is there, and I make a note to transfer the cash to Jane's account when I get home.

"The colors reflect emotions," Martha says, finally dropping her shirt and sitting down across from me.

"Nifty," I say, although in all honesty it sounds like they've run out of cheap mBedis worth having and can't afford the major stuff like Hovertiles. It's basically a cosmetic mBedi with a twist. Boring.

"Everyone's getting them," Jane says, but Martha kicks her under the table so she adds, "I mean, not everyone, but we saw Allison and Doug in line behind us, and Trevor looked super jealous when we ran into him in the coffee line. He says he's saving up."

Martha gives me a sly look. "Even Matt was there," she says.

At the mention of Matt, my face gets hot. No mBedi needed to interpret that. "Do they have to go in the stomach?" I ask.

"Some of the guys are getting them on a bicep, if they have room," Martha says. "You want it to be visible, you know?"

"Definitely for Allison's party tomorrow night," Jane says. I want to point out that their typical t-shirts aren't exactly see-through, but I have a feeling they plan to remedy that for tomorrow—either with scissors or a wardrobe change between home and the party.

"Let's go together," says Martha, and even though she's being nice, that suddenly sounds like a nightmare. Everyone from school, showing off their mood mBedis, while I'm stuck with the ability to text my mother or offer directions. Which everyone else has, anyway.

I jump out of my seat and the chair tilts against my knees, threatening to crash to the floor. "I gotta go," I say. "I'll see you guys tomorrow."

"You just got here," Jane says.

"Sorry."

I know they're watching me leave, and that they'll put their heads together and gossip for the next hour about whether a lack of mBedis leads to brain damage or something, but I don't care.

I head straight for the mBedi store.

VAL'S LEANING against the glass when I get there. She pretends not to see me until I'm right in front of her, though there aren't many other people around and she has to have been waiting for me.

"I didn't think you'd show," she says.

"Then why did you?"

She shrugs and pushes off the wall. "I get a cut. Let's go. Not often I get to show up with an mBedi virgin."

"I've got the mandatory ones," I say, defensive.

Val doesn't answer, which is worse than another sarcastic comment. Maybe she doesn't want to lose a customer by harping on the brutal truth.

The unlicensed mBedi parlor isn't far from the main store. We wind down a side street and a narrow set of stairs that lead below street level, and we're there. If you were to glance down while walking on the sidewalk, you'd just make out the decal in the window and the sad collection of tattoos they pretend to do. It's a front, which any official should know; why would anyone get tattoos? There's an mBedi for that, and you can change them.

There's no jingly bell on the door or anything, but as soon as Val slips inside a skinny guy comes out of the back. His head almost brushes the low ceiling, and he's wearing a sleeveless shirt so I can see he's got more mBedis than I've ever seen on one person. He's a walking Times Square. He's got round nano mBedis on each earlobe, and a bunch more just below his knuckles. I've never understood what a screen that tiny can offer—nail polish, maybe? Hand moisturizer? He's got various sized screens all up and down his arms, some of them black, others alive and flashing.

"New blood?" he asks, looking me over.

"This is Richie," Val says. "Richie, this is—I don't know your name."

"Laurel."

"Well, Laurel, Richie's the best unlicensed mBedder in the city."

Richie holds out his arms and spins a circle. "Did most of these myself."

The mBedi store has tiles and walls to display their products; this place has Richie. "Nice," I say.

"What're you here for?"

I've got enough for a Hovertile—not like I've got anything else to spend my allowance on—but I'm not licensed, and those controls have to go on a hand or arm, where Mom would see. I take a deep breath. "Can you do the new mood mBedis?"

Val twists her lips in distaste, but Richie claps his hands together. "I can do anything, doll. Have a seat."

I'd thought Val might take off, but she slides onto the counter to watch as I sit on the edge of the chair. It's like a dentist's chair—which people with dental mBedis have no reason to know about, lucky them—and after he measures my stomach, Richie tips the chair back. "Ready?"

I nod, even though I'm way more nervous than I thought I'd be. I grip the arms of the chair while Richie shoots me with a local anesthetic. I try to relax. Every once in a while I sneak a glance at what he's doing, because I figure it's probably easy to go too deep with a stomach mBedi or to kill someone by sticking the wires in the wrong place. I keep expecting a to feel a jolt or a jab to my stomach, maybe even an electric shock. In some ways it's even weirder that I can't feel much at all.

After about an hour, Richie steps back with a grin that makes his cheek mBedis look like overdone rouge on a clown. "All righty," he says, "your current mood is relief. Gnarly."

I look down at my stomach, where the skin is rimmed in gentle red around the brand new screen. The mBedi shows waves of blue-green, not exactly calm and yet somehow exactly reflective of the relief I'm feeling now that this is over.

I pay Richie, and Val escorts me out of the shop. "I don't know why you'd want to show off your feelings for everyone to see," she says.

I'm not sure I do, either, but I just thank her and head for home.

IN THE MORNING, the anesthetic has worn off enough to make moving pretty painful. My whole abdomen is sore, which I guess makes sense. I know my friends have felt some discomfort after their new purchases. Martha and Jane were still on the anesthetic when I saw them yesterday, so I'm actually looking forward to sharing that part of the process, almost as much as I'm looking forward to seeing the look on their faces when I show them what I got.

I do my best to hide the mBedi while I'm making breakfast, but Mom watches me from behind her coffee mug like I'm some kind of a weirdo. Maybe it's because I wince as I reach for the toaster.

"Did you hurt yourself, Laurel?"

"Yeah," I say. "Overdid the sit-ups. Don't forget I have Allison's birthday party tonight."

For all the credit I don't give her, Mom's smarter than that. She narrows her eyes, but I'm wearing an over-sized sweatshirt and as far as I know, she isn't licensed to be mBedded with x-ray vision.

Still, I change quickly and head off to school early, with my toast, before she decides to investigate further.

Martha and Jane are duly surprised by my transformation, and we decide to go shopping for cropped shirts before Allison's party. Neither of them seems to be in pain, and I don't want to ask because even though they know I'm a newbie, it's important to be a non-dull newbie. There's no redness around their mBedis, and mine's still pink at the edges. They don't mention it, so I figure it's nothing to worry about.

I'm feeling pretty rotten by the end of school, but there's no way I'm wasting my first real mBedi by missing Allison's party. We go shopping together and pick out the same shirt in different colors—a strip of cloth to cover the boobs, with a curtain of tassels hanging over the midriff. My first choice is blue, but Martha wants to match today's highlights so I end up with green instead.

When I strip my shirt in the dressing room, there's an oozing situation starting at the corner of my mood mBedi, but I doubt anyone would notice but me. The screen swirls with sickly yellow and orange worry, but I ignore it, try on my tassel shirt, and get dressed without showing the girls how it looks.

Allison's having her party on the roof of some important building. The doorman even checks a list and draws lines through our names before we're allowed to go up. I'm lucky that Jane and Martha have kept hanging out with me through the years. If they didn't stick by me, I'd never get invites to this sort of thing.

The party is packed with people and dark like a dance club, with multicolored searchlights figure-eighting across the floor. Leafy trees grow everywhere, like it's half-park, half-roof, and strings of lanterns droop over our heads. When we get closer, I see that each lantern is made of cube-shaped screens playing slideshows with pictures of Allison. Clusters of people stand near the low ones in the corners, giggling at the poof of a ponytail she had in elementary school.

Jane and Martha link arms, so I join them. We're a trio, with Martha in the middle. With my legs feeling shaky, Martha's arm through mine is solid. Like a reinforcement. They let go when we reach the dance floor, and I do the same, reluctantly.

We dance. Jane and Martha's mBedis are matching kaleidoscopes of color, spinning droplets of confidence and joy.

When I glance at mine, it's giving off half-hearted yellow and green swirls. Nerves and lightheadedness. Great. At least no one can see the oozing edges in the dark.

And then Matt dances up beside us.

"Ladies," he says, and something in my stomach drops. Like there's a mini roller coaster in there, and I just went through the loop.

Matt's the kind of guy who already looks like he's been spending most of his time learning how to do whatever his parents' business is—stocks, securities, I don't know. He wears a button-down shirt over long khaki shorts, his brown hair perfectly parted on one side. Unlike the other boys in our class, he knows how to recognize and operate a comb. He's got a tasteful number of mBedis, and is drinking something brown in a short glass, which only increases the impression of his maturity.

"You look tan." Martha's tone is accusatory, like 'you look like you're up to something,' only it's 'your skin looks more golden than normal.' I'm not sure how she can tell, since it's pretty dark up here.

"Just got back from the islands," he says.

Then he looks at me. He glances at my stomach and grins. "You ever been, Laurel?"

"Uh, no," I stammer. "I'd like to."

"Clearest water you've ever seen."

I smile, trying to think of something clever to say. Did you see any starfish? No, too specific. Did you go snorkeling?

"Hey Laurel," Jane says, sounding too casual, "maybe we should go get a drink."

I want to shoot her a what-the-hell look for interrupting, but then I catch a glimpse of my mBedi's reflection in Matt's glass.

Hearts. Red and pink hearts, swirling around the screen in a huge spiral. I drop my gaze to the horror, unable to comprehend how this could be happening. The hearts pop like little bubbles, and the remains turn into swarms of more hearts. Smitten. My mood is smitten?

Jane's effort to save me is wasted when Matt's eyes follow mine to the mBedi. He gives me a little smile and backs up, arms raised in mock surrender. Then he melts away into the party while the people around us start to laugh.

I abandon the dance floor and push my way toward the elevator. I'm feeling woozy, and the mBedi is back to yellow, mixed with harsh red embarrassment. Jane and Martha follow, even when I blow through the lobby and the doorman says, "No reentry!" Somehow, their stomachs are still pulsing with that beautiful kaleidoscope, and I realize the mood mBedis are as full of shit as everything else. You must be able to freeze them on a happy emotion or something.

I want to accuse my friends of setting me up, but as soon as we reach the street I fall to my knees on the curb and wretch. Jane grabs my hair, and Martha puts a hand on my shoulder as the world turns into spots.

"Oh my god," Martha says, "look at her stomach."

"We have to get her to—"

Where? I wonder.

The lights go out.

A FEW DAYS after my release from the hospital, I stop by the mBedi store. I'm extremely grounded, probably more grounded than anyone has ever been, in all of history. But I'm well within my school-to-home-travel-time limit, and this won't take long.

Val's scrubbing a tile in the courtyard when I get there. I walk up and stand over her, letting my shadow fall right on top of the square she's working on. She looks up, annoyed.

"What?" she says. "Looking for another mBedi?"

"Not since the last one almost killed me, thanks."

She doesn't need to know my body's decided to reject all

mBedis. Even my messages and map have shut down, and no one can say if I'll be able to use them again. "Sealed your own fate, kiddo," Mom said when the doctor outlined the prognosis—which basically amounted to "we'll have to wait and see." Which basically forced me to inform him that medical school may have been a waste of time in his case.

I guess, though, that Mom's not *totally* wrong about the sealing my fate thing. Jane and Martha aren't talking to me, and I'm starting to think it wasn't the mBedis that edged us apart over the years. I'm not sure I can win them back. I'm not sure I deserve to.

Val's eyes go all big, and she looks at my stomach. I can see her doing the math—there's obviously no mBedi outline beneath my shirt. "You didn't rat on Richie, did you?"

I shrug. "Couldn't say. I was heavily medicated."

Val gets up, shoves her rag into her back pocket, and stalks into the store without another word. I assume she's going to call Richie. I also assume the police will have raided his shop by now.

I'd love to stand here and savor the moment, but I've got a curfew to keep and no way to message Mom that I'm running late—not that she'd buy any excuse I have to offer.

It's always been weird to have fewer mBedis than everyone else. Now, it's downright lonely.

Maybe someday, when I'm favored for gold in Olympic Hovertile, the announcers will tell my story with awe in their voices, describing this incident as the most appalling setback I could have been forced to overcome. *Yet here she is,* they'll say, *about to make Hovertile history.*

As I walk home, I daydream of surfing on the wind.

YOU ALWAYS HAD A THING FOR SILVER LININGS

When the sky first changed, I thought it was pretty. Champagne gold, like a gift. Like a Bond villain decided on the color. The more I look at it, the more I think it's actually the vomit of some alien race that decided to use Earth as a trash can.

Could be.

No one expects to be around for the Last Day.

All those apocalyptic movies, they got a few things right. Like the cars jammed onto the freeway, which is where I like to do my picking. All it takes is a jimmy with a coat hanger to get me neck-deep into most trunks, stashing bottled water and canned goods in my pack.

What the movies missed? The silence. I guess that's because someone always saved the day before this point, so they never had to imagine the absence of that oh-so-human electrical hum, the water moving through pipes.

Weirder still is the absence of birds cawing and pecking, the rustle of cats in the garbage, the growl of dogs, the skitter of cockroaches (surprise! we thought they'd outlive us, but if they did, they've gone dark).

At least it's easy to sleep late.

Once you said, What if I were the last man on earth? Then would you want to...you know?

And I said, What's the point? Am I horny, or...?

You said, Repopulation, and I said You know, I never understood that, because if you're the last man and I'm the last woman, then our children would have to...*you know*... with each other in order to continue humanity, and we're not exactly hamsters.

And you said, OK, you're horny.

Now I'm spread out on the hood of a dead SUV, tucking canned peaches under the facemask that sorta-kinda protects my nostrils from the smell of decay. The peaches are too close to the color of the sky.

The sun filters through the sickly atmosphere like fluorescent light through cheesecloth, and I'm trying to figure out what I should do tonight.

If you were here, would I change my mind? I'm pretty sure that by tomorrow, there'll be no world to repopulate. Not enough time to fertilize an egg, baby.

Let's say *that* is off the table.

What would you have wanted to do on your last night, if you'd had a few hours to choose?

Video games. Food.

I could find you a board game, probably, and dinner's taken care of. Hello, peaches.

There's a hot pink iPhone on the passenger seat of the SUV, earphones coiled as if lying in wait. I've long since stopped feeling guilty about looting, but still, I almost leave it. What do I need an iPhone for?

Still, I hesitate.

I pop open the door.

The iPhone has juice.

You used to sing that old Drifters song, as if it might change my mind.

This iPhone belonged to someone young, because the singers are all Jessee and Kellee and Chad. No Drifters, no Frankie Valli.

What made her leave it behind?

I check the earphones for wax before getting off the highway. I skip down the exit ramp, pretending it's a slide. I should have found a town with a waterpark. Or I bet I could have made it to Disney World. So what if the rides wouldn't run? I'd have climbed the rungs of the roller coasters, just to sit at the top. I'd be lounging on Dumbo to eat my peaches. I'd be sleeping in Cinderella's castle.

I'd be wearing Mickey Mouse ears. No, Minnie.

The sky is getting too bright to look at, like a sunset gone wrong.

The park has the fewest bodies, which I know because I was the one who moved them. I drop my pack beneath a tree. There's no one to steal it, nothing to rip it apart for peaches.

You'd hum it under your breath: Save the last dance for me.

Thanks for reading!

Join my newsletter to get a free story collection, plus access to my VIP-reader library! Join here:

https://katesheeranswed.com/free-books/

Also by Kate Sheeran Swed

League of Independent Operatives

Alter Ego

Anti-Hero

Mastermind

Nemesis

Defender

Toccata System Novella Trilogy

Parting Shadows

Phantom Song

Prodigal Storm

Complete Trilogy Box Set

(includes bonus short story)

Short Stories

Don't Look Back (And Other Stories)

For information on my other work, including my young adult titles, visit katesheeranswed.com.

ABOUT THE AUTHOR

Kate Sheeran Swed loves hot chocolate, plastic dinosaurs, and airplane tickets. She has trekked along the Inca Trail to Macchu Picchu, hiked on the Mýrdalsjökull glacier in Iceland, and climbed the ruins of Masada to watch the sunrise over the Dead Sea. Kate currently lives in New York's capital region with her husband and son, and two cats who were named after movie dogs (Benji and Beethoven). She holds an MFA in Fiction from Pacific University.

You can find more of Kate's work, and pick up a free short story collection, at katesheeranswed.com.

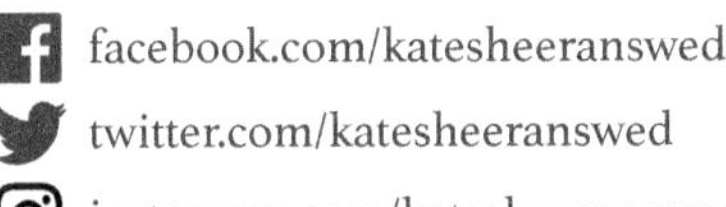